Miranda
and the Movies

by Jane Kendall

with illustrations by the author

Crown Publishers, Inc. New York

Library of Congress Cataloging-in-Publication Data
Kendall, Jane F.   Miranda and the movies / Jane Kendall.   Summary: The arrival of a band of moviemaking visionaries in peaceful Leewood Heights enlivens the summer of 1914 for twelve-year-old Miranda. [1. Motion pictures—Fiction.]   I. Title.
PZ7.K334Mi   1989   [Fic]—dc19   89-1515

ISBN 0-517-57301-6

ISBN 0-517-57357-1 (lib. bdg.)

10 9 8 7 6 5 4 3 2 1

First Edition

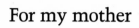

For my mother

Contents

Acknowledgments

This book was no solitary effort—despite the title page—and I owe much to many: Esther Mitgang lit the initial spark, Allen Atkinson and Luisa Viladas fanned the flames, and the talented and dedicated people at Crown made everything pleasurable and exciting. My deepest gratitude goes to my editor, David Allender, for his unswerving belief in the book and for his skill, patience, and humor.

My thanks to Mary Corliss of the Museum of Modern Art Film Stills Archive and to The New York Historical Society for invaluable photographic research; to Abigail Kweskin for posing as Miranda with vivacity and charm; to director/film historian Charles Turner—my "film school"—for generously lending material from his collection and running films at a moment's notice; and to Leatrice Gilbert Fountain for opening doors with enthusiasm and for graciously allowing me to cast her mother, silent screen star Leatrice Joy, in an unbilled cameo as the Fort Lee cowgirl.

I am forever indebted to Thames Live Cinema for the rich, overwhelming experience of seeing silent films as they were meant to be seen, and to Kevin Brownlow's *The Parade's Gone By . . .*, the book that opened my eyes to the glorious adventure that was pioneer filmmaking.

Finally, although this book is meant as fiction—not film history—any juggling of dates and data was done after much agonizing, in the spirit of the Jack London quote: "Make it vivid. Truth doesn't matter so much, so long as it lives."

Miranda
and the Movies

Moving Day

Miranda was sprawled across her bed reading *The Count of Monte Cristo* for the fourth time when the truck rumbled down the street and stopped in front of the empty house next door. She paid no attention. She was just coming to her favorite part, where the star-crossed lovers meet after twenty years, and she knew if she concentrated on every word she could work up a good flood of tears. It was all too tragic . . . it was all too romantic . . . it was—

"Holy sufferin' cats!" bellowed an unmistakably Irish voice. "Watch where yer puttin' that crate, will yez?" There was a screech of splintering wood, and a crash shook the branches outside the open window.

The Count would have to wait. Miranda put the apple core she'd been nibbling in the book to mark her place, climbed down off the bed, and ran to the window. By leaning out as far as she dared, she could see a battered green van pulled up to the curb. The tailgate had been let down; a large wooden crate had tipped off the ramp and lay half in the street, one end torn outward. The contents were spilled into the dust.

Strewn at awkward angles among the packing straw and newspapers were—dead bodies! Three or four, she thought excitedly, and an arm.

Miranda pulled herself back over the sill and ran out into the hall. Grabbing the banister, she tore down the stairs two at a time, rounded the newel post with a glorious swoop, and hit the landing with a thump that rattled the bric-a-brac in the glass-fronted cabinet. She stopped, one foot poised over the next step, and whispered, "Cutthroats!"

"Miranda!"

Miranda did not answer. "Or maybe axe-murderers," she whispered, eyes shining. "Of course. Who else would have corpses? Oh, I'll just bet they're here to hide out and bury their victims in the lot down the street. I'll jus—"

"Miranda Louise Gaines!"

All three names required an answer. "Yes, ma'am?"

"You walk down those stairs like a lady and stop all that hooligan noise."

"Yes, Auntie." Miranda listened for a minute, but there were no further commands from the parlor. She tiptoed down the rest of the stairs, and across the hall to the front door. Turning the big glass knob slowly so it wouldn't rattle, she opened the door and looked out. All clear.

She was at the elm by the front gate in one dash. She flattened herself behind it, palms pressed against the bark; when her chest stopped heaving she peered around the trunk.

A man was standing over the broken crate, mopping his forehead with an immense blue bandana. He was well over six feet tall, and heavyset. His reddish hair was dark with sweat, but the walrus mustache winging into two waxed curls over his cheeks was as bright as a new penny. Beside him a tall thin boy with dark hair was crouched in the street, picking up the scattered straw.

The bodies had vanished. I'll bet they put them back in the box, Miranda thought. All squished on top of each other.

The boy tossed a last handful into the broken crate, stood, and wiped his hands on his dust- and sweat-streaked shirt. "I'm sorry, Jerry," he said. "I guess it was heavier than it looked. Kinda got away from me."

"No harm done, lad." The man laid a friendly hand on the boy's shoulder. "And a fine thing, too—Mary'd a had my hide if anything'd happened to them mannykins a hers."

Mannykins? Miranda puzzled. What're mannykins? Oh. . . . She slid down the trunk and sat in the grass with her legs straight out. Dummies, she thought. Like the one Aunt Lucy uses for dressmaking, I'll bet.

"Why aren't we unloading in back anyway?" the boy asked.

"Oh, you know His Nibs," the man chuckled. "Rented a van wider'n the drive. Let's give 'er another go. Got a grip, now? And one . . . and two . . . 'n' up she goes."

Miranda pulled a blade of grass and chewed the end as she watched Jerry and the boy lug the crate down the drive between the houses and out of sight. I guess I wouldn't really want murderers next door, she thought, but there sure isn't anything interesting about sewing dummies . . . not even a whole trunkful.

Just thinking about sewing made her cross; she and Carrie spent rainy afternoons drawing page after page of the most sumptuous ballgowns, but would Auntie ever make her anything grown-up? No, it was middy blouses and plain skirts and those awful Sunday dresses, and endless fittings in the little room off the back porch. Auntie would scuttle around her on the floor, tugging and snipping and muttering through a mouthful of pins, "Stand up straight, for heaven's sake. And quit that fidgeting." And Miranda would stand until she was sure she was going to faint, and think of Tommy and Jimmy off playing baseball or Cowboys 'n' Indians without her— and fidget all the more.

She stood, and looked down at her skirt. Grass stains again. Auntie would not be pleased. She walked back up the front walk,

scuffing the toes of her high laced-up shoes against the bricks. Sewing dummies . . . nothing interesting ever happens around here, she thought. This is 1914, for Pete's sake, not the Dark Ages. Right across the river from New York City and a lot of good it does me. We might as well be in the middle of nowhere.

She trudged up the front steps and flopped down on the porch swing. In winter the wide front porch was merely a place to dump snow-caked boots, but summer brought it to life: wicker chairs deep in chintz cushions, tables piled with magazines and books, and, ranked in stands, hanging in baskets, marching along the railing, the plants liberated from the parlor.

"Nothing ever HAPpens, nothing ever CHANges," she chanted, timing the words to the squeak of the swing as she stared out at the street. It's always the same, she thought glumly. You play with girls when it rains and boys when it doesn't, and the games are always the same. And when you don't feel like playing you read your favorite books over and over again. You get a picnic on the Fourth of July—and you never get enough firecrackers—and your birthday to look forward to, and Christmas. You get a new teacher every fall and that's . . . about . . . it.

The shadows were lengthening under the tall trees lining Pine Street, and lights were starting to come on in the houses. Mrs. Duncan came out onto her front porch wiping her hands on her apron and screamed, "Jimmy!" The response came high and thin through the dusk: "Co-o-m-i-i-ng. . . . " Carrie's father walked home along the narrow board sidewalk with the evening paper folded under his arm; he tipped his straw boater and called out, "Good evening, young lady," as he passed.

"Good evening, Mr. Fellowes," she answered politely. Almost time for supper, she thought. Oh, I hope we don't have peas again. She went inside, letting the front door slam behind her.

Miranda's aunt was in the kitchen at the back of the house. With her neatly round figure, sugar-pink and blond coloring, and

swift, practical manner, Lucy Browning Gaines resembled an animated china figurine. "There you are," she said. "Wash your hands, darling, then fetch me the pitcher of tea from the icebox."

Lucy had set the table in the windowed alcove next to the pantry. (The dining room was only for Sundays, or for what she called "state days and bonfire nights.") The striped curtains were drawn, and the lamp in the center of the table cast a cozy glow over the oilcloth covering. After they were seated and grace had been said, she asked pleasantly, "Have a nice afternoon?"

"Yes'm," Miranda replied. "I saw some people next door."

"Mmmm. Maybe the place's finally been rented. I do hope you'll be considerate, darling, and let the new people settle in before you descend on them."

"I just saw two people unloading a truck," Miranda said. "I don't know if they're the new neighbors. A man and a boy—he looked older'n me. They had a trunkful of dummies and it broke because they dropped it and then they picked up the dummies and that was all, I guess."

"Dummies, plural? With all the dressmaking I do I need only one. You must've been mistaken."

Miranda speared a pea on the end of her fork and regarded it sadly. "At least seven or eight," she sighed. "And an arm."

"Lordy, Miranda, where do you come up with these things? That is just plain foolish. And stop staring at that pea, it won't bite you. Have you learned your verse for Sunday school?"

"Yes'm." Miranda looked down at her lap.

"Well, help me with the dishes—you dry—and then I want to hear it before bed." Lucy looked over at the bowed head. "Come here a minute." Slowly, Miranda scraped back her chair and walked around the table. Lucy placed the back of a hand on the girl's forehead. Cool and dry. "Sweetie, what's wrong?"

Miranda stared at the floor and bit her lower lip. "You won't just laugh and say I'm silly?"

"Of course not. What is it? Is something wrong at school?"

Miranda shook her head.

"Have you been fighting again?"

Miranda glared at her, and again shook her head.

"I'm not a mind reader, Miranda."

Miranda wound her fingers in her blouse and thought, Oh please, don't let me cry, oh please—and it all came tumbling out in one big rush. "Oh, Auntie, I'm sorry, I know it's stupid but I just can't help it, I just know it. . . ."

"Know what, for heaven's sake?"

"That nothing's ever gonna happen to me. Not here. I'll just do—oh, I don't know—what I'm s'posed to and be like everybody else and die of boredom and—and—and never get to go anywhere and I . . . oh . . . nothing is fair!" she ended on a wail.

"I don't think you're silly, darling," Lucy soothed. "Spring fever, that's all it is. Spring fever and that imagination of yours. Of course you think nothing is ever going to happen to you. I thought the very same thing when I was your age."

Miranda stared morosely at her. But nothing ever did happen to you, she thought. You just lived in the same old town forever and taught piano and made dresses.

"Oh, enough of this, Sarah Heartburn," Lucy said as she rose from the table. "Enough, enough. Help me clear. Besides, there's only, what, one week of school left? Then the whole summer to do as you like, play with your gang, go swimming. You'll forget all this gloom and doom then, I know you will. And who knows, darling? Maybe the people next door'll be interesting."

Huh! Miranda thought crossly. In Leewood Heights? I'll just bet. She carried a plate across the kitchen and stood looking out the window over the sink. The sheets hanging on the line glowed white and luminous against the twilight. Like the sails on a Spanish galleon, she thought, rounding the Horn with a hold full of smuggled treasure. Gold doubloons and pieces of eight. Maybe I'll run

away to sea. I could cut my hair and be a cabin boy.

Miranda Dantes, cabin boy *par excellence*, drew her sword to defend herself against the villainous advances of the hook-fisted Jamaica Jake, Scourge of the Seven Seas. The plate fell to the floor.

"Miranda!"

Under the Window

Every Sunday the women gathered in front of the church after the service. They clustered beneath the trees dotting the broad green lawn, laughing and gossiping while they waited for Sunday school to let out, or for the men to finish swapping tall tales in the courtyard. The breeze chattering through the leaves overhead set the ribbons on their wide straw hats dancing, and whipped their long skirts into a creamy foam around their ankles.

When Lucy came out of the church Emma Duncan was waiting for her at the bottom of the steps. "We have to talk," she hissed into her ear and, hand firmly under Lucy's elbow, steered her across the lawn.

"One hundred and twenty-nine yards of unbleached muslin and canvas," Katherine Fellowes was saying to Pearl Stowing, for the third time. "I do not understand it. Every inch of the cheapest white fabric in the store. Marcus said the woman paid cash."

Emma drew her lips into a tight rosette and leaned forward. "I know what's going on, girls—and you are simply *not* going to believe it."

"Don't leave us hanging, Emma," said Pearl. "Out with it."

"Well!" Emma settled her bag on her arm and folded her hands together. "Lester Jackson—down to Leewood Realty, you know—told me he rented out the Macdougall place."

"Oh, is that all?" said Lucy. "Miranda said she saw some people moving in yesterday."

"People?" Emma snorted. "They're not people, they're actors! *Actors*. And Lester gave them a lease for the whole summer; business sense of a donkey, that man. Can you believe it? Show people in our town! They bought all this lumber over at Dieterle's, and Rose Dieterle told me that the man who bought it—some brute the size of a tree, she said—told her it was for a stage. And I—"

"Maybe all that muslin was for curtains," Katherine interrupted. "But why build a theater on our block? It doesn't make a whole lot of sense."

"Let me finish, Kate," Emma said darkly. She drew herself up and looked around at the three women. "These people are much worse than common theater folk. They're in the *moving picture* business, if you can call that disgusting claptrap a business. They make flickers. Cheap awful comedies. 'Slapstack,' I think it's called. All summer long they'll be carrying on right under our noses, tramping through my flower beds, stirring up our children with their sinful ways. What are we going to do?"

"Why do we have to do anything?" Pearl said. "If they're here to make flickers don't you think they'll be too busy to bother us?"

"Besides, Emma," Lucy added, "there are some perfectly respectable actors: Maude Adams, the Barrymores. They're not all as wicked as you say."

"Pearl, you never did have the sense God gave a goose," Emma snapped. "And as for you—" She turned to Lucy and said coldly, "I should have known better than to expect your cooperation. And we all have good cause to remember why, don't we? When I think of the grief you caused your poor mother, God-rest-her-soul."

Katherine gasped. There was an uncomfortable silence, and

Lucy turned her head away and looked out over the lawn. When she turned back her face was pale. "For heaven's sake, Emma," she said quietly. "That was twenty years ago."

Pearl patted Lucy's arm and said, "A little Christian charity, Emma, please. It *is* the Sabbath. Why don't we find out how bad these people are before we start casting stones."

"Fine," Emma said sourly. "Stand there and defend actors if you so choose, but let me remind you, girls—" She paused until all eyes were on her. *"One of them shot Lincoln."* She took her gloves from her bag and pulled them on, shoving the kid down over her plump fingers as she continued: "A house divided cannot stand. We must unite against this viper in our bosom. Do we want our dear little children exposed to a bunch of no-account trash— Oh, it's you, Miranda. What do you want?"

"Nothing, ma'am," Miranda replied. "Sunday school's over, that's all."

"Come along, darling," said Lucy. "Let's go home."

"Oh, Lucy dear?" Emma said with acid sweetness as they turned to leave. "I think we should continue this discussion after dinner. Shall we say three o'clock? Your house?"

"If that's what you want, Emma," Lucy said without turning her head. She took Miranda's hand and they walked away.

"What was all that about, Auntie?" asked Miranda as they walked down Broad Street, past Duncan's Grocery Emporium and the high school. "I could hear Old La—Mrs. Duncan yelling halfway across the yard."

"Nothing for you to concern yourself with," Lucy said absently. "Nothing at all."

"Well, then hurry up," said Miranda, tugging at her aunt's hand. She could hardly wait to get home, finish dinner, and change out of her Sunday best. Every week she tore through the lovingly prepared meal, gulping down her milk and stuffing in the chicken and biscuits as rapidly as propriety allowed.

"Sunday ought to be called Button Day," she fumed, sitting in

her window seat while she laboriously worked the buttonhook up the sides of her white kid boots. She untied the wide ribbon sash around her hips, tossed it on the bed, and set about unfastening the twenty-four tiny pearl buttons up the back of the starched organdy dress. "I'm s'posed to be thinking about Jesus and being good," she muttered, "and all I can think about is getting out of these darn clothes."

When Miranda went back downstairs, comfortably dressed in an old skirt and blouse, she found Lucy standing at the kitchen table talking to herself. "That stuffy old cow, who does she think she— Lordy, Miranda, don't sneak up on a person like that!" She took the lid off the fat china cookie jar, banged it down on the table, and started arranging butter cookies on one of the good plates.

"Is that for your meeting, Auntie? Are you planning a party?"

"Not exactly," Lucy said grimly. "I think you'd better play outside this afternoon."

Miranda stood solemnly on one foot and hopped up and down. "Jimmy 'n' Tommy," she puffed, "are going somewhere and said I couldn't come and Carrie 'n' Nell only ever want to play dolls and I'm . . . too . . . old . . . to . . . play . . . dolls."

Lucy opened a drawer and started counting out tea napkins. "Then go play in the backyard or walk around the block or something. And stop that, you made me lose count. Shoo!"

Miranda left the kitchen and crossed the back porch. She wrapped around the edge of the screen door and swung back and forth. It was warm for the end of June, and still. The breeze had died; the only sounds in the lazy air were an occasional bird trill, and faint snatches of ragtime from a player piano in the next street. At the Macdougall place a screen door slammed and a loud laugh rang out.

Miranda jumped down, retraced her steps, and peeked into the kitchen. Lucy was standing with her back to the door, humming "I Wonder Who's Kissing Her Now" and cutting paper-thin slices of bread for tea sandwiches. Every so often she would break off,

whisper something, listen for a moment, and whisper a response. After watching for a minute Miranda decided she was rehearsing an argument—a sure sign Old Lady Duncan was on the warpath again.

She tiptoed back across the porch, slid through the door, and, crouching low like an Indian brave, slunk across the yard. She circled the high yew hedge between the houses and crossed the drive, stepping over the strip of weeds down the center. She reached the side of the house and straightened up, heart pounding. Made it! she thought, and nobody saw me.

Miranda had never been inside the shabby gray clapboard house. Angus and Hilda Macdougall had been elderly, private, and unreceptive to noisy children; the previous winter they had gone to Ohio to live with a married daughter. Miranda had peered in the windows a few times since then, but broken chairs and odds and ends scattered on dusty floors were not much to look at. The adjoining lot had always been more intriguing, anyway. Once the Macdougalls' garden, it had been left years before to weeds and neglect. The surrounding wall lent an air of mystery, and the wormy, inedible apples from the ruined orchard made excellent ammunition.

Clinking sounds and voices were coming from around back. Miranda sidled around the corner of the house and knelt behind the hydrangea bush by the kitchen window. A door slammed somewhere in the house and heavy footsteps crossed the room, stopping at the open window above her head.

"Ah, me darlin', despite C.J.'s what-he-calls help, the boys'll have the stage up in a coupla days."

The stage? Miranda put her hand over her mouth so they could not even hear her breathe (eavesdropping was not only rude, it was forbidden). A stage? she thought. They're building a theater? I could just die!

"Oh, Jerry," a woman's voice replied. "We scarce get here—

haven't even finished unpacking—and he's got you all slaving away like navvies."

Who's that? Miranda wondered as she edged closer to the window. Jerry's the one I saw yesterday, the big man with the curly mustache, but who's he talking to?

"What's in the pot?" Jerry said.

"Irish stew—and you can take that 'not again' look off your big ugly face," the woman laughed. "It's cheap and it's filling," she went on, "and it'll put meat on your bones. Not that you need it, mind, but if there ever was a body needed fattening up it's that poor sweet Gilmer boy."

"Sh-h-h-h. Shush now, he's in the next room. He'll hear you," Jerry whispered. "He's a good lad and he's got his pride—too much, maybe—and y' know he don't take to motherin'."

Miranda heard a noise that sounded like a spoon banging down on the stove. "Oh, he's independent enough, I'll grant you," the woman said in a low voice. "Been on his lonesome since he was thirteen. Well, maybe after a coupla years now he's used to it—acts so free 'n' easy, like he expects nothing from life—but it's not natural. If you ask me, under all that clever talk he's just a poor motherless lad who could use some looking after. At least you can't stop me from feeding him!"

The big man laughed affectionately; Miranda heard a smacking sound and the woman said, "Get off with you while I'm cooking."

I think he kissed her, thought Miranda. Maybe they're married. They certainly sound married.

"At it again, you two?" said a third voice, a light, friendly voice.

"Just a little sugar, lad, just a little sugar," said Jerry. "Why don't y' take yer nose outa that there see-nario and go have a look at the set? C.J.'s got 'em all poundin' away like billy-o."

"Maybe later, Jer'," said the voice. "I want to finish some notes. The more we get done the less chance there'll be for Mrs. McGill to kick a fuss . . . or C.J.," he said.

Is that the boy I saw yesterday? Miranda thought. The one she called Gilmer? It sounds like him, and he was awfully thin.

"Mi-raaaaan-daaaaah."

Oh, Auntie . . . just when it's getting good. She unfolded herself and ran swiftly across the overgrown yard. From the kitchen window of the old Macdougall place the slender dark-haired boy watched the girl run through the tall grass, her flying red braid catching and throwing back the sunlight as she disappeared around the hedge.

" 'M home, Auntie."

"In here, darling."

Miranda trotted down the hall to the parlor. The heavy brocade drapes had been looped back over the lace curtains beneath and the late afternoon sun was shining amber rectangles across the Turkish carpet and glinting rainbows through the prisms on the china-shaded lamps. Lucy was stacking plates and collecting napkins from the marble-topped table in front of the davenport. "Help me carry these to the kitchen," she said, "and then I have to talk to you about something."

Miranda followed her down the hall, chattering all the way: "Oh Auntie, oh Auntie, I have to talk to you too. You're not gonna believe it, you're just gonna die it's so wonderful." She set the plates on the scrubbed pine table in the center of the room, sat herself on it with one joyous bounce, and kicked her legs straight out. "And I thought nothing was ever gonna happen around here," she sighed ecstatically. "Guess what, Auntie? Guess what?"

Lucy sat at the table in the alcove and observed the sparkling eyes and flushed cheeks. "Oh, darling girl," she said heavily. "Listen to me, please. It has to do with our new neigh—"

"I know, I know," Miranda interrupted. "They're building a stage—a real live theater!—right down in the lot. Maybe they'll want someone to play piano for the shows, you could—"

Lucy stopped her with a raised hand. "Sweetie, come over here and sit by me." Miranda jumped off the table and ran to the alcove.

Lucy smoothed her linen skirt over her lap, closed her eyes briefly, and took a deep breath.

"This is serious," she began. "Those people next door—yes, they are, it appears, building some sort of theater. I will not repeat, certainly not to you, what I consider to be gossip, but most people feel that—" She paused. "These people are not for us. They—"

"Why is that, Auntie? Mrs. Duncan is always saying things like that. 'Theater people are trash, Miranda,'" she mimicked in a mincing voice. "But she never explains why."

Lucy looked over the girl's head and spoke slowly, choosing her words with care. "Theatricals live differently. Most people think they are . . . morally unfit. Not decent. They may seem enticing and even thrilling to you—I daresay, knowing you as I do—but they are considered a bad influence, especially on children. They don't live the way we do. They go where they want, from town to town like gypsies. Like the raggle-taggle gypsies. . . ." Her voice trailed off, and she pulled her handkerchief from her sleeve and dabbed her eyes.

"Aunt Lucy?" Miranda leaned over and scrutinized her face. "Are you all right?"

"Of course," Lucy said thickly, and blew her nose. "Hay fever. Oh, honey, these people aren't even ordinary theatricals. Apparently they make moving pictures." She fingered the cameo at her collar. "Flickers."

Miranda's eyes widened and she sat bolt upright. "Golly," she breathed. "Like Mary Pickford? I heard about her."

"Well, dear, no. Not quite like that. Nobody Emma talked to had ever heard of this outfit. Oh, that doesn't matter. None of it matters, except what I have to tell you. The house next door, the old garden lot, the moving picture people—darling, they're all off limits. Forbidden territory."

"Was that what your meeting was for?" Miranda demanded hotly. "Deciding I can't make friends with them, or have any fun?"

"Oh, Miranda," Lucy said wearily, shaking her head. "Why

must you always be so dramatic? Not just you. Tommy, Jimmy, the Fellowes girls, all the children around here. This decision has been made for . . . for the good of the community, and for reasons I will not go into we have to abide by it. If you disobey me you will be punished."

Miranda slumped back, sullenly kicking the chair rungs. This is the most unfair of all, she thought. Something finally happens in this town—right next door, for Pete's sake—and I can't be a part of it? I wanted to make friends with them, especially that Gilmer. Rats.

"Miranda? Miranda, pay attention," Lucy said firmly. "You promise me you'll stay away. Now."

Miranda hid her hands under the sides of her skirt and crossed her fingers; she crossed her big toes over too, just for good measure. "Yes, ma'am," she said sweetly. "I promise."

Lucy looked at her sharply. "So help me Hannah, you better mean it," she said, crossing her arms over her chest. "You know very well I'll be too busy with dressmaking and my teaching schedule to keep an eye on you. Eleven—oh, all right, almost twelve— is too young to be left on your own so much, but it can't be helped. You have to be a good girl, darling. I have to trust you on this."

"You can trust me, Auntie," said Miranda. "I won't get into trouble." I won't get into trouble, she thought, really I won't. And I did cross my fingers, so it doesn't count. I could just take a quick look around and not talk to anyone. . . . One little look couldn't hurt, could it?

Up a Tree

Miranda spent the next week in a state fluctuating between the paralyzing fear that she was headed for trouble, and excitement so enormous she felt it should have been visible in the air around her like a cloud of colored smoke.

The walk to school each morning was devoted to the summer ahead, as ripe with promise as found money. Despite Miranda's vivid—and repeated—assurances of adventures to come, none of her friends seemed interested in the Macdougall place or its unsavory tenants. Tommy and Jimmy schemed and argued over their plans for "the best fort Leewood Heights has ever seen"; Carrie and her little sister Nell nattered on and on about the dollhouse their father was building in their attic playroom. Miranda answered "Yes" and "I'll bet" and "That sounds like fun," but all the while her mind was screaming: "Flickers! Moving pictures!"

In school she daydreamed, leaning on her hand and staring glassily at the blackboard. She thought about the friendly-sounding Irishman and his wife, the amused way in which the unknown C.J. was discussed, the tantalizing danger of a theater right down the street—and "the motherless lad." It's about time there was another orphan 'round here, she thought, 'cause I sure am sick of being the only one.

Orphanhood was a sore point with Miranda, and it had nothing to do with self-pity. Orphans had terrible reputations, either as peaked little waifs like Oliver Twist, or nauseating goody-goodies like Little Lord Fauntleroy or Pollyanna. Being an orphan meant ladies patted you on the head and made sad clucking noises and called you "poor thing." Now, suddenly, "orphan" meant a mysterious boy who lived on his own and did as he pleased.

All week the block rang with the racket from the walled lot: hammering, banging, sawing, yelling, raucous laughter, and, occasionally, music. Most of the neighbors shrugged their shoulders and closed the windows. Emma Duncan, however, was furious.

She burst in on Lucy midweek, sat herself down in the parlor, and demanded refreshment. "I've been everywhere," she panted, "and no one in this town will so much as lift a finger." She held out a pudgy hand. "Look at that. Shaking like a leaf. My nerves are in shreds. Shreds . . . oh, thank you, dear." She took the proffered cup of tea, sipped primly, and sank back on the davenport. "Well, aren't you going to say anything?"

"I don't know what to say, Emma," Lucy replied. "I have no idea what you're talking about."

"Those heathens and their hammers! I went down to the courthouse this morning, and was handed some mumbojumbo about 'being within their legal rights to build.' I ask you. So I tried the police station, but Archie Stowing told me they weren't breaking any local ordinances and I 'shouldn't get my bustle in an uproar.' I told Pearl not to marry that man, but would she listen?"

"Now, Emma—"

Emma plowed on: "You know, Lucy dear, that I take it as my civic—my sacred—duty to root out evil from our happy little community. Someone had to tell those people we don't go for their sort of folderol, so I marched myself right over to that lot and knocked

until this man opened the door—" She fanned her face with her hand and moaned, "Never in all my born days. . . ."

Lucy folded her arms and sighed. "What did you do?"

"Do?" Emma said huffily. "I didn't *do* anything. I barely got started when this man—some dreadful little bald fellow in a riding getup—screamed at me to get myself to a nunnery and slammed the door in my face! Whatever do you suppose he meant by that?"

"I'm sure I don't know," Lucy replied evenly. "Anyway, I thought the whole point of our meeting was to keep everyone away from them. If they want their privacy it solves everything, doesn't it? I have noticed they've not tried to introduce themselves around much."

"I know," Emma snapped. "Have you ever heard of anything so rude? And my Hobart says if their money's good we have to serve them in the Emporium. Me, waiting on theater trash! It'll take every ounce of strength I have just to be polite to them."

"Yes," said Lucy. "I can see that."

And, after telling her tale of woe to anyone who would listen (and some who wouldn't), Emma took to her bed. "She's not sick, Auntie," Miranda reported. "Jimmy says she got his dad's binoculars and spends all day in a chair by her bedroom window watching the street. Jimmy says like she was expecting spies or something."

"I expect she'll stop when she realizes there's nothing to see," Lucy answered. "You have been obeying me, haven't you? Just stay away from those people, darling. It's for the best."

"Oh yes, Auntie," this with a quickly averted face. "I have much better things to do."

On the Saturday that spelled freedom Miranda awoke early. She pulled the covers over her head to shut out the morning sounds of doors and calling voices and milk bottles clinking onto porch steps, and went over her plans for The Great Secret Expedition. She could not include the gang; they might try to talk her out of it, or, worst of all, they might tell on her.

She waited until midmorning when Lucy was safely in the par-

lor, shepherding her students through their lessons from a straight-backed chair beside the massive ebony Steinway. Miranda did not envy them. She, too, had spent painful hours squirming on the piano bench, squinting at the profusion of notes that had to be transferred to the keys. Auntie always said "a well-brought-up young lady must play the piano," but it was awfully hard to practice when she would call out from the kitchen: "B flat, Miranda, B *flat.*"

After securing provisions suitable to a great explorer (two bread-and-butter sandwiches and an apple stuffed into her skirt pocket), Miranda slipped out the back door. She went directly to her spot under the Macdougalls' kitchen window, but a few moments' listening told her no one was home; an empty house had its own resonance, a hollow kind of stillness.

The backyard of the Macdougall place was bordered on the east by the yew hedge and the Gaines property, on the north by a tangle of bracken and underbrush leading to the pine woods beyond, and on the west by the old garden lot. The yard sloped up to meet the fence; from behind it came the familiar cacophony of raised voices and construction noises.

"They're all there," she whispered exultantly as she crept across the yard. "I'll bet they're in the theater."

The weathered gray fence was at least six feet high, and Miranda knew from past attempts that the splintery boards could not be scaled without a leg up. The door in the fence had been warped shut for as long as she could remember, there was no door in from the Fellowes property on the opposite side, and the Pine Street door was right across from Old Lady Duncan and her spyglass. There was a gate into the woods, but the fence along the back was only waist-high. How can I investigate in secret if they see me coming? she thought, chewing a thumbnail. Maybe I could dig a tunnel, or—

Miranda looked down the fence toward the woods. There stood the answer, grown tall by a century of sun and rain—the perfect climbing tree. She walked over to the scarred old maple, looked up, and noticed that one thick branch jutted over the fence.

"If I can get out on that," she said aloud, "I can see what they're doing and they won't see me. I won't even be breaking my word 'cause I'll just be climbing a tree, not talking to anyone."

Miranda was one of the best tree-climbers around, a skill more appreciated by her friends than her aunt. She spat on her palms and rubbed them together, took a deep breath, and ran straight for the tree. The speed sent her scrambling up to the lowest branches. She clung there panting, then swung herself up onto the next branch. The apple fell out of her pocket and bounced to the ground. Grunting with effort, she braced her feet against the trunk and pulled up onto her goal. The branch was broad enough for her to crouch on all fours; she inched forward until she had passed over the fence, then glanced down.

"Uuh!" she gasped. The ground sloping up to the fence fell away just as sharply on the other side. She was frozen—fifteen feet in the air, gripping so tightly her hands and knees ached, scarcely daring to breathe. She waited until the sick feeling in the pit of her stomach abated and her heart stopped banging in her ears, then swallowed hard and looked down again.

Where's the theater? she wondered. I don't see anything that looks like any theater I ever saw.

The scrub pines and saplings at the back of the lot had been cleared to make room for a curious structure. A platform had been constructed, covering an area as wide as Lucy's parlor and twice as long. Telephone poles had been raised at the corners and at regular intervals along the sides; a complicated cat's-cradle of wire had been strung between the tops. Long lengths of white cloth laid over the wire grid made a semitransparent roof twelve feet above the floor.

Work was in progress somewhere at the back of the platform. The cloth roof prevented her seeing anyone, but that was where the banging and hammering noises were coming from.

The front half of the platform had been partitioned into small, boxy rooms. (Like Carrie's dollhouse! thought Miranda.) One sec-

tion appeared to be a dining room. A round table and four spindly chairs were set on a rumpled piece of patterned carpet, and the flimsy board-and-canvas walls were a painted imitation of wainscoting and striped wallpaper. The adjacent cubicle was the inside of a barn; there were two stalls, tools and harnesses hung on the painted walls, and a layer of hay on the floor. The room at the end of the platform resembled a stone cell in a medieval dungeon. "Ooh," she whispered, "like the Chateau d'If in *The Count of Monte Cristo!*"

Immediately below Miranda was a garden shed. It was only six by eight feet, but for reasons known only to the Victorian mind of Angus Macdougall had been fitted with a pitched roof, a Dutch door, and one four-paned window. Long abandoned, it had served as a clubhouse, as the fort in a long-running game of Cowboys 'n' Indians, and, on one memorable occasion, as the Tower of London.

Miranda crawled forward until she could see over the edge of the roof. Her former haunt had been transformed into a rustic country cabin. Yellow gingham curtains had been pinned up in the glassless window and behind the top half of the door. A small front porch had been attached, and two rickety chairs were set in the narrow space behind the railing. A short flight of crudely built steps led from the center of the porch to the grass.

A half-dozen people were gathered in a semicircle around a man who stood with one foot cocked up on the bottom step. He was perhaps forty, of a stocky, muscular build, and at least a head shorter than Jerry. His costume was simple and dashing. Cavalry boots burnished to a chestnut sheen were laced over flared whipcord riding breeches, a paisley silk scarf was knotted around his throat, and the sleeves of his loose white shirt were rolled to the elbows. Miranda could not see his face. The top of his head was bald and sunburnt, and the remaining blond hair was cropped short. Carefully, she leaned down to listen.

"We'll set up here, my children," the man was saying in a rich, plummy tenor. "Can't be helped, and I do hope this lovely sun lasts.

Those cretinous fools should have finished the interiors by now, but—" He shrugged and someone laughed. "Now, I want you, Miss Dulcinea, and you, Robert, on the porch here." He gestured grandly to the chairs. "Indulging in a few stolen moments of ever so bucolic love . . . aah, Love!"

"Mrs. McGill?" He turned to address a tall, hawk-faced woman who stood, with a proprietary air, beside a delicate blond girl. The older woman appeared to be in mourning: her unfashionably cut suit, buckled shoes, handbag, and gloves were black, the jewelry at her throat and ears was jet, and her black straw toque was draped with heavy black veiling. "We shall procure a chair for you so you may take comfort whilst we toil." He spoke with such frosty courtesy that Miranda could tell he did not like her. Not one bit.

He paused, and found Jerry standing patiently at the back of the group. "Donnelly, let's break tradition and start with a middle-ground shot for this setup. Waist up and no roof, so come in to about—oh, seven or eight feet. You judge."

"Right-o, C.J.," Jerry said briskly.

So that's C.J., thought Miranda. What on earth was he talking about? And where's Gilmer? I don't see him anywhere. . . . She crouched back onto her heels, and managed to get into her pocket for the sandwiches. The climb had not improved them, but she downed them hungrily as she watched the activity unfold.

Jerry was setting up a machine several yards away from the shed, handling it as though it were both heavy and delicate. The main part was a plain black box—just over a foot high, just under half a foot deep—upended on a circular platform of levers and gears. The back of the box was tricked out with dials, doors into the mechanism, and a short knob-tailed handle; a round glass lens fitted with a metal collar protruded from the front. A long, narrow wooden box was affixed, lengthwise, atop the black box. It was divided into two square sections; a round of metal was exposed in the center of each. The entire contraption was mounted on a structure that looked like three crutches, spread open so the top of the machine

came to Jerry's chin. Not that she had ever seen one, but Miranda decided if it was a machine and it was aimed at the shed, well, then it had to be a moving picture camera.

When Jerry was finished he called out, "Bring them reflectors over here, boys." Two swarthy men in coveralls dragged large white canvas-covered wooden frames across the grass and set them between Jerry and the shed. He peered through a square tube mounted on the side of the camera, and guided the workmen until sunlight angled off the canvases toward the porch.

The two actors had taken their positions. Dulcinea played with her long blond sausage curls, arranging them on her shoulders. She wore a sprigged pink muslin dress frilled at the neck and wrists, the fluffy skirt caught up here and there with knots of ribbon. Her wide Leghorn hat was trimmed with ratty-looking artificial flowers, and tied under her chin with green velvet streamers.

Robert slouched back in his chair with angular grace and whistled tunelessly through his teeth. Miranda thought he was wearing too much clothing for a warm June day, but it didn't seem to be bothering him. Over a plaid wool shirt buttoned to the chin he wore a shabby tweed jacket patched at the elbows. The long legs were in faded denim overalls, the feet propped casually on the railing in heavy bump-toed work boots. His black hair was slicked back from a side part with brilliantine and, although she could not see his face clearly, Miranda thought he had a mustache.

C.J. was striding up and down talking to himself, nimbly dodging the crew. Mrs. McGill sat behind and to the left of the camera, her contribution a running commentary: "Watch where you're putting that, young man, that was almost my foot. Dulcinea, Mother sees a loose hair on your cheek. No, left. That's better. Stop lounging, Robert. Mister Tourneur, I'm sure that hat will shade her face. We have to see her face—"

Finally, although it was a barely perceptible break in the chaos, they were ready to begin. There was a portable Victrola on a small table near Jerry. C.J. took a record from the stack on the ground,

put it on the turntable, wound the handle, and set the needle. The scratchy strains of "When You Were Sweet Sixteen" floated out of the battered tin horn, adding to the confusion.

"Quiet!" he roared.

Suddenly, miraculously, the noise level dropped.

He put a short leather-covered megaphone to his mouth and bellowed, "Roll camera!"

Jerry bent over and started to turn the handle on the back of the camera, muttering rhythmically as he cranked: "One hundred and *one*, one hundred and *one*, one hundred and *one*. . . . "

A young man in a grubby cap and baggy pants ran to the front of the camera, missing the outstretched tripod legs by inches. He held a writing slate with numbers chalked on it directly in front of the lens, yelped, "Scenefourtakeone," and ran behind Jerry.

C.J. yelled "A-a-and . . . action!" He began to stalk back and forth, pitching his voice over the music and the grinding of the camera and the construction noises still coming from the back of the lot. "You're in love," he wheedled. "You have finally found some time to be alone. Finally, despite the wishes of your horrible families, finally alone. Together, my children. Dulcinea, My Sweet, put your left hand on Robert's shoulder. Good. Now gaze up into his face. Tilt your head back, we're getting too much hat. Look at him, lo-o-ok at him—ah! what rapture. Robert, look down at your beloved. Tenderly, you clot, *tenderly*."

Swept into the scene by the tension and the music and that imperious voice, Miranda crawled forward. The people beneath her were completely concentrated on the task at hand; no one thought to look a few feet above the top of the shot where a bright-eyed girl crept along the branch, her thick red braid swinging down over one shoulder.

"Aah, yes," C.J. continued. "Now, Miss Dulcinea, pull away from Robert. Just a touch, just a touch. You are shocked, ever so slightly, at the ardor of your young swain. You fear discovery, you—"

Miranda was now directly over the porch. She inched forward again, not noticing in her absorption that the branch narrowed. She grabbed for it and missed, her hands smacking together over empty air.

"No, oh no!" she shrieked. She grabbed desperately, reaching out to fasten around the thin whipping twigs where the branch feathered into leaves. Her feet scrabbled frantically for a purchase on the slick bark. "Aaaaaaah!" she wailed—and fell.

Down she went, right onto Robert. She rolled off his lap, careened off the porch railing, and tumbled head over heels down the stairs. She crashed to a stop in front of the bottom step, lying on her back in the grass with one arm flung out.

The last thing Miranda heard before everything swam into mist was the trail of broken twigs that rattled down in her wake—and the sound of surprised laughter.

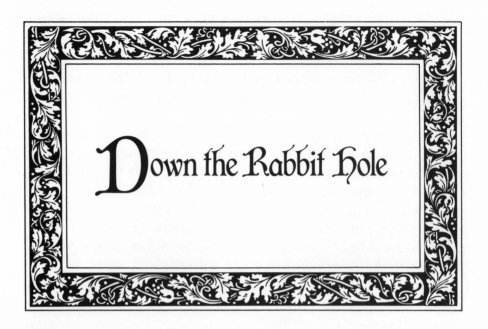

Down the Rabbit Hole

"Little girl. Little gi-i-i-irl. Hey, kid, wake up—you're scarin' us." There were voices buzzing over her, around her, and someone was gently shaking her shoulder.

"Mmmpf . . . 'm up. I'm up, Auntie," Miranda mumbled.

"Hey you!" a voice yelled against her ear; Miranda opened her eyes. Green eyes heavily rimmed with black stared into hers. The face not three inches away was a ghastly yellowed white, a coarse black mustache glued above its bright purply-red mouth. "Yaah!" she shrieked, squeezed her eyes tight shut, and rolled away.

"Come back here!" A hand grabbed the hem of her skirt. "It's okay, Red, it's okay."

Miranda stopped wriggling and opened her eyes again. Robert was bending over her. "Your face," she whispered. "What happened to your face?"

"Oh, Lor', it's the makeup," C.J. guffawed. "Nothing to be afraid of, child—though I must say if I awoke to some buffoon looming over me like Banquo's Ghost 'twould give me pause. And who, pray tell, are you?"

"Miranda Louise Gaines," she whispered. "Sir."

"Any bones broken, Miranda Louise Gaines?"

Miranda sat up, felt her arms and legs gingerly, and shook her head. "No, sir."

"Sorry I scared ya, Red," said the actor. He smiled down at her, a wide, crooked smile lifting one corner of his mouth. "M' name's Robert," he said, "but most everybody calls me Bobby. Bobby Gilmer."

Miranda looked up at him, then stared—under all the paint was her mysterious orphan! With that mustache and that slicked-down hair he sure looks older than fifteen, she thought, and not so skinny in those clothes. He called me Red . . . I like that.

Still smiling, Bobby put his hand out. "Howdoyoudopleasedtomeetyou," she said faintly, and reached up to shake hands. He grabbed the hand and pulled her to her feet.

For one mad moment Miranda thought they were all playing Statues. Jerry had stopped cranking the camera and leaned on it, chin in hand. Dulcinea had fled the porch and stood beside him, shoulders heaving, straw hat askew. A dark-haired woman who had been sewing by the fence had run over to them, thimble on her finger, thread dangling from her mouth. Even the workmen had left off their muttered stream of imprecations, and stood behind the reflectors staring at her.

She felt the warmth rise in her cheeks, and dropped her eyes from the circle of faces. I'm in trouble now, she thought miserably. Maybe if I run for the gate—

C.J. walked up and glared down at her, arms crossed. "And now, Miss Miranda Louise Gaines, would you be so good as to explain why you were doing as fine an impersonation as I have ever seen of Alice falling down the rabbit hole? Hmmm?"

Miranda swallowed, and looked up at the round face. Despite the firm tones his china-blue eyes twinkled.

"I was only climbing a—I was explor—" She stopped and thought, Oh, you might as well tell the truth. She straightened up

to her full height, drew back her shoulders, looked him square in the face, and said, "I wanted to see what you all were doing. I—I was snooping."

"Delicious! Honesty strangely becoming in one of your tender years. That's what I thought you were up to, anyway." His shoulders shook and the stern demeanor dissolved as he started to laugh, generous booming laughter that seemed to roll right up from his boots. "Oh, Lor'," he gasped after a minute, and pulled the scarf from around his throat to wipe streaming eyes. "If you could've seen yourself! Flying, bouncing off Robert, all elbows and knees. I shouldn't laugh—it's a bloody miracle you didn't crack your skull—but oh, oh, it . . . was . . . rich!" He wheeled around. "Donnelly! When did you stop cranking?"

Jerry stroked his mustache and replied, "Not 'til after the lass hit the ground, Boss. Took me by surprise, she did."

"Hmmmm. Interesting." C.J. put an arm around Miranda's shoulders and led her over to the others. "Introductions, dear girl," he said expansively, rolling his *r*'s. "We are The American Moving Picture Company. I am Charles James Tourneur, known to all and sundry as C.J., director, Indian chief, and the, ahem, artistic genius behind this motley band of players. Mr. Gilmer you have met. Despite his somewhat obvious youth he is our Leading Man—when I can get his face out of a book and in front of the camera where it belongs, that is." He moved her along the line. "This Son of the Old Sod is Mr. Jeremiah Donnelly, cameraman *extraordinaire.* Also film cutter, developer, tinter, and sometime security guard." He traced a flourish in the air, and ended in a pose that reminded Miranda of the picture of Enrico Caruso Aunt Lucy kept on the piano.

"Atcher service." Jerry saluted the cap he wore with the bill turned to the back, and smiled down at the pair.

"This enchanting vision," C.J. continued, "is our Leading Lady, Miss Dulcinea Josephine McGill." The volume dropped, and his

voice went husky. "Fashioned by the gods from moonbeams and rose petals. Sent to Earth for us poor mortals to kneel before in wonder and adulation . . . Our Dulcie."

Dulcie glanced nervously at the woman in black, then smiled merrily at him. "Oh, Charlie, how you talk." She turned to Miranda and took the girl's grubby hands between her soft white ones. "Are you sure you're not hurt?" she asked anxiously. "You frightened me so."

"I'm fine, really I am," Miranda said. "I've fallen out of trees before, lots of times." I've never seen anyone that pretty before in all my life, she thought. She looks more like one of the illustrations in my Rackham fairy tale book than a real person. I wish my hair would curl like that.

"This is Dulcie's mother, Mrs. Bessie McGill," he said, and nodded curtly to the woman.

That's perfect, too, thought Miranda. She looks just like the Evil Fairy at Sleeping Beauty's christening. "How do you do, ma'am." She ducked her right foot behind her left, as she had been taught, and bobbed a quick curtsey.

"You ruined my daughter's scene," the woman said coldly.

"Oh, Mamma," said Dulcie. "Who cares as long as Miranda wasn't hurt?"

"Puh," snorted Mamma into a black-bordered handkerchief.

"Hello, dearie. I'm Mary Donnelly, Jerry's wife." The dark-haired woman leaned over and kissed Miranda's cheek. "We are all," she said pointedly, "very pleased to meet you."

Oh, Auntie, you were so wrong, thought Miranda. How could people this nice be a bad influence on anyone?

"Now, children." C.J. rubbed his hands together briskly. "This is all very well and good—this moppet is by far the most charming creature yet encountered in this benighted backwater—but we don't want to lose the light, do we? Right. Miss Miranda, why don't you sit with the Mistress Donnelly while we finish. Or would you

rather assume your former perch in yon tree? No? I thought not."
He chuckled as he retied his scarf. "We'll pick it up from just before
Peter Pan's entrance."

"Al, Tony," he called to the men in coveralls. "Go work on the
interiors, boys. You, too, Georgie," he said to the fellow in the
grubby cap. "Jerry can slate the rest of the takes. We're just going
to reshoot 'til the light goes. If those sets aren't done when the
generator and the Cooper-Hewitts get here—"

"There'll be the devil to pay," grumbled one workman, and the
other muttered, "Nah, just him."

Miranda went over to Mary, seated in a scarred kitchen chair
in the shadow of the fence, and sat in the grass at her feet. She
pulled her knees up to her chin, pulled her skirt down to her ankles,
and hugged her legs. She tried to figure out what C.J. meant, but it
was more perplexing than French class. That Mr. Tourneur certainly is clever, she thought. I do feel exactly like Alice and Peter
Pan, all rolled into one, as if I'd flown into the Mad Hatter's Tea
Party or dropped into Never-Never Land.

Mary took a button from a tin box on her lap and began to sew
it to a shirt with rapid-fire stitches. Jerry's wife was short, sturdy,
and pretty in a simple, country way, with frizzy brown hair twisted
into a coil at the nape of her neck. She was adorned only by the
tools of her trade: straight pins on her shirtwaist, tape measure
around her neck, scissors tucked into her waistband. The Company's costumes hung behind her on a row of nails in the fence. The
glory of the collection was a blue wool policeman's uniform, almost
new and with most of its buttons. The rest were merely serviceable;
threadbare shirts, trousers, and calico farm dresses, faded, patched,
and stained with makeup and dried rings of sweat.

She bit off the thread and glanced at Miranda; the girl was
wrapped into a tight ball, and her dark eyes were slightly glazed. "I
can imagine," Mary said, smiling, "that you don't quite know what
to make of all this. It's a treat to watch, though. That's why I bring
my work outside when I can."

"I feel like I can't breathe," Miranda whispered.

"Well, you did have the breath knocked out of you," Mary said. "I'll tell you a little secret. I felt the same when I met this crew a few years back, and I didn't fall out of any tree! Got used to 'em in time, though."

Oh I want that chance, I do, thought Miranda. A yearning so intense it tightened her throat and made her chest ache swept through her. *I want this,* she thought, I want to be here more than anything I ever wanted. . . . Running away to sea or crossing the Alps in a balloon or riding in a Wild West show—all her pet fantasies—seemed childish by comparison. To belong, in any fashion, to these people and this entertaining confusion was suddenly the most important thing in the world.

C.J. finished placing Bobby and Dulcie back on the porch, and, after a hurried conference with Jerry, strode over to the Victrola. The record had long since ended, ignored in the drama of The Girl in the Tree. The needle was emitting an endless *sssclick . . . sssclick . . . sssclick* at the end of the band. He reached for the stylus, paused, and called to Miranda, "As you have caused this magnificent enterprise to come to a halt—midflight, as it were—how would you like to make amends?"

Miranda scrambled to her feet: He wants me to help!

"Can you work a gramophone, a Victrola?" he asked.

"Only since I was five," she answered promptly, "I'm not a baby, you know."

"Child! A curse be on my house would I ever accuse you of such a thing," he said. "So how old are you?"

"Twelve, sir. Well, eleven and eleven-twelfths. I'll be twelve in August."

"A splendid age, I'm sure. Come with me." She followed him over to the little table, and he pointed to the stack of records in the grass. "Keep those coming until I say 'cut.' "

"Does that mean stop, please?" Miranda asked shyly.

"Good! Better to ask than operate under a cloud of pigheaded

assumptions, I always say. Simple, really—'roll camera' starts Donnelly cranking, shooting the scene. On 'action' my darlings commence acting their tiny hearts out. 'Cut' indeed stops each 'take.' Some say that's all one need know to direct, the fools. Anyhow, you pay attention and keep the music flowing like rivers in the spring."

"Can I—I mean, may I pick it out myself?"

"Don't see why not," the man said, "provided you bear in mind we're not shooting "The Charge of the Light Brigade." He arched one blond eyebrow. "Right?"

"Right-o, Boss," she said boldly.

C.J. laughed, feinted a slow punch to her chin, and returned to his pacing path beside the camera.

Miranda rifled quickly through the well-worn records, relieved to find most of the titles familiar. Romantic ballads like "Shine On, Harvest Moon" and the lilting waltzes from the operettas Aunt Lucy loved so would do nicely; "The Anvil Chorus" and John Philip Sousa she put to one side. She stood tensely over the Victrola, winding it up at the merest hint of flagging speed, grabbing from her stack the moment each song ended. The melodies wafted over the lot, adding to the curiously satisfying disharmony composed of conversation, construction, and C.J.

The wooing on the porch continued. Every time Bobby tried to get close to Dulcie she would turn away demurely, fiddle with the streamers of her hat, or flutter a dainty hand up to her face. On one take Bobby smacked a loud kiss on the brim of her hat and lost his balance, catching himself clumsily on the railing. C.J. slapped his thigh and roared, "Great touch, deah boy!"

Miranda noticed that whenever he directed Dulcie, he watched even the smallest reaction flit over her lovely face with a kind of hunger. "Lean over her, boy," he would call out to Bobby, and would lean in with him, unconsciously mirroring the movement. Bobby was acting out the rituals of courtship, but C.J. was living them. And, as the afternoon wore on, it became increasingly ap-

parent that the biggest barrier between the director and the actress was not six feet of grass and a megaphone—it was the dour presence of Madame McGill.

She observed the action with gimlet eyes, interrupting whenever the directions were too impassioned: "Mr. Tourneur, if you please. I will not have Dulcinea associated with that kind of racy material. That is not the image I want for her."

"Rest assured, Madame," C.J. said with rigidly controlled frustration. "We are making a gentle rural romance, not some lurid drama of sin and retribution. Booth Tarkington, Madame, not Henrik Ibsen. We will charm the audience, not drive them screaming into the streets." With precise language and exaggerated diplomacy they wrangled. Dulcie kept quiet, as did Bobby; they had long since learned not to engage in the running battle.

The afternoon wore on, take after take, frame after frame of film looping past the lens. The initial thrill had abated, but Miranda was not the least tired or bored. She watched intently, every nerve attuned to the mellifluous voice that begged, cajoled, whispered, roared.

When the sun dipped behind the trees, Jerry announced, "Light's gettin' yellow, Boss."

"All for today," C.J. called out. "We don't want to lose your precious faces." The actors rose stiffly and came down from the porch. Dulcie stood limply, rubbing the back of her neck. Bobby walked in circles like a racehorse cooling down, shaking out cramped hands and feet.

Jerry wrapped a ragged army blanket around the machinery, collapsed the tripod into a long bundle, and heaved the camera up onto one broad shoulder. "See ya later, gang," he called back as he headed down the lot to the street entrance. "Gotta get me darlin' Baby back to the house an' unload her."

C.J. walked over to Miranda. "Still at your post? A veritable Boy on the Burning Deck, you are."

"Do you—" Miranda looked up at him and said, "May I please come back and help you again?"

"So you find all this foolishness to your liking, do you? You ridiculous child, of course you may," he said. "Why would I want to fire my new musical director? You know," he put an arm around her shoulders and went on confidentially, "many companies have live music, a trio usually, to create the mood. Our funds, however, do not extend to such largesse. I suppose you charge an exorbitant fee for your services?"

"No, sir," she said earnestly. "Being here is enough for me."

"Child, child—I jest! You're welcome here any time, as long as you do as I say and don't get in our way."

"Yes, Boss," she said happily.

"You've got the day off tomorrow. We don't shoot on Sundays, as a rule. The McGills come over from the City, you know, and Madame refuses to let Our Dulcie work on the Sabbath. A regular Big Bill Heywood, that woman. Smaller mustache, though."

"Uh-huh." She nodded, thinking Big Bill Who?

"You live nearby, presumably," he stated.

"Yessir," said Miranda, abruptly on shaky ground. Aunt Lucy's voice sounded in her head: *Stay away from those people . . . It's for the best . . . You will be punished.* "I live—in town."

"Well then, ask at home if you can come out and play. We don't want to incur the wrath of the local bourgeoisie, sterling citizens though they may be." He fingered his chin, thought for a moment, then said suspiciously, "Your mother isn't by any chance a round little woman with a small mouth and a large temper, is she?"

"No, sir. She—"

"Splendid!" He clapped her shoulder. "Monday it is."

She went around and said her good-byes, then headed toward the back of the lot. "Bright and early, now!" C.J. called, as she opened the gate in the north fence.

She meandered along the path, turning in dizzy circles, throwing her head back to watch the pines spin overhead. "I can come

this way on Monday," she said to herself. "Auntie'll think I'm going to play in the woods or go down to the river, and the flickers people'll just see me come out of the woods. They won't know I live right next door."

She reached her backyard and walked around Lucy's vegetable garden; each row staked, labeled, and weeded with the same orderly attention she gave to buttonholes, or Bach. She swished aimlessly through the cool grass and, deep in thought, crossed the back porch and went into the kitchen.

"Hello, darling," said Lucy, peeling potatoes at the sink. "I swear I don't know why some folks make their children take piano in the summer. I had three boys today with fingers sprained from baseball. I hope you had a better day than I did. What did you do?"

"Nothing much, Auntie," Miranda answered. "Played some, listened to music."

"That's fine, darling, that's fine."

The Moving Picture Game

Miranda had a terrible time getting to sleep on Sunday night. Every time she closed her eyes the excuses she had been fabricating all day jumbled through her head, clanging and echoing and bumping into each other. She finally drifted into a light, troubled sleep; the first bird trill at dawn opened her eyes as if a switch had been pulled.

She got her well-thumbed *Monte Cristo* from under the bed, read until the nightstand clock said quarter to seven, then slid out of bed and tiptoed into the bathroom. It was a slapdash toilette; she made one swift pass with the washcloth and tossed it in the direction of the towel bar, knocking the can of tooth powder to the floor. It skittered under the claw-footed tub, dusting white plumes across the tiles. "Later," she panted, "I'll clean up later. I can't be late my first day," and she ran back down the hall.

Trembling with excitement, she fumbled her hair into a braid, yanked up her cotton stockings so hard one ripped, and tried to put her head through the armhole of her slip. Button the skirt, drop the middy blouse over her head, and she was dressed—but she laced her shoes so rapidly she missed half the eyelets and had to start again at the bottom. The quilt thrown over the rumpled sheets, a perfunctory poke to the pillows, and she was out and clattering down the back stairs.

Lucy was leaning against the kitchen table, listlessly grinding coffee beans. "What in heaven's name are you doing up and dressed at this hour?" she said. "You're usually a slugabed in the summer."

"I—uh—the river. I thought I'd go down to the river. It's—it's such a beautiful day I didn't want to waste any of it."

"That sounds lovely, darling," Lucy said, tipping the grounds into the coffeepot. "I have fittings all morning—Jenny Alden's coming by for another go 'round on her wedding dress—then lessons all afternoon." She retied the sash of her flowered wrapper and said, a little sadly, "I don't know when we're going to have any time together."

"Oh, Auntie. It's not so bad. We have supper every night, and Sundays together sometimes."

"You're right, darling, so we do. Sit down and I'll fix you a proper breakfast. What would you like?"

"Just cereal, please. The cold kind." Who had time for a hot breakfast?—there were flickers and music and people waiting.

At seven-thirty Miranda dashed out the back door, raced through the woods to the lot, and threw open the back gate with a big smile. The lot was empty. She walked around the platform stage and peered into the dim cubicles, calling "Hello? Hello, is anyone there?" but the only reply was the rustle of the muslin drapes swaying in the morning breeze.

Bright and early, my Aunt Fanny! she thought, and circled back through the woods to the Macdougall place. The hedge blocked the view from her house, so she walked straight to the back door and knocked. She could hear conversation and laughter in the kitchen.

Bobby Gilmer opened the door and grinned at her through the screen. "Hmmfhng, Rmmf," he said, and swallowed the mouthful of scrambled eggs. "Morning, Red."

"Who disturbs our blissful peace at this ungodly hour?" bellowed C.J. from inside.

"It's Red," Bobby said over his shoulder.

"Does she wish to use the door or would she prefer to climb the roof and drop down on us?" he called out.

She heard Mary say, "Oh, Charles, you wear a joke to the fraying point," and C.J. chuckled, "Can't help it. Best laugh I've had in years."

"Enter at your peril," said Bobby, and he held the door open.

A speckled enamel coffeepot burbled sweetly on the wide black stove, sending out the wonderful aroma that mingles so well with frying bacon and toasting bread. The kitchen was flooded with light from the uncurtained windows. There was the usual stove, icebox, and woodbox. The only furniture was an enormous oak hutch against the far wall and a large round table surrounded by mismatched chairs. C.J. had commandeered the largest, a dilapidated wing chair upholstered in a taxing shade of purple brocade. The stuffing protruded in several places and one arm was missing, but he sat in it as if it were a throne.

"Come join us!" he said heartily, waving a piece of buttered toast at her. "Mistress Donnelly has prepared a most Lucullan repast."

"Thank you, I already ate." She sat on the broken-backed rattan chair next to Bobby, and looked around the table at the four faces. "You're all staring at me again," she said uncertainly.

"Bear with us; there is a method to our madness," C.J. said, and turned to Jerry on his right. "Features aren't bad. So-so mouth—a little wide—but her nose is good, short and straight. Nice heart-shaped face, firm chin. Brown eyes, mercifully."

"No problem with the film pickin' those up," agreed Jerry, "but d'ye think the little darlin' can act?"

"Hey!" Bobby interjected. "Stop talking about Miranda as if she weren't here."

"I stand corrected," said C.J. "Shocking lapse of manners." He leaned over the table, scarf ends trailing across his plate, and said, "First things first. We're here to work, not tangle with the natives, so I must be certain your presence will cause no problems. Any objections from your parents?"

Miranda looked down at her lap. "My mother and father are dead. They died when I was three. Typhoid."

"Oh, the poor little thing," said Mary. Bobby looked up from his plate and stared at her.

C.J. toyed with his fork and cleared his throat several times. With uncharacteristic gentleness he said, "Who do you live with, my dear?"

"I live with my aunt, sir," Miranda said, not meeting his eyes. I hope they swallow this, she thought. "She's real old and real crabby and sick most of the time, so she doesn't much care what I do . . . I mostly take care of myself."

She raised her eyes. C.J. and Jerry looked concerned and sympathetic; Mary had tears in her eyes. Bobby was leaning on the table with his chin resting in his hands, gazing at her with an unfathomable expression. Miranda looked back down at her lap.

"I ask," said C.J., "because we had a conference yesterday after we ran the footage of your descent. Robert and I came up with what we think is a peach of an idea. Look at me, child."

Miranda raised her head. A generous smile lit his face. "How would you like to be in our picture?" He beamed.

"Me?" she squeaked. "In the flickers?"

"Yes, you, you wide-eyed little innocent. And please—flickers is what you call those cheap outdated nickelodeon things. We make moving pictures!"

"I'm sorry," Miranda said quickly. "I didn't mean to insult you. Most people 'round here say 'flickers' and—and I never saw a nickelodeon."

"Y' didn't miss much," Jerry said. "Them things was ages ago. 'Fore the pictures grew up, y' might say."

"I'll say," agreed Bobby. "At least five years ago. And weren't they just awful?"

"Prehistoric bilge compared to the modern photoplay," said C.J. "Remember, Donnelly? Standing in a dreary storefront, ankle-deep in cigar wrappers and tobacco spit, turning the handle and peering in at that dim little screen . . . and what was your reward? Magic tricks older than Methuselah, or some poor cooch dancer utterly unsuited to her profession. And what passed for theaters? Throw a few chairs in the back of the druggist's on Saturday night and you were in business. Remarkable, really, when you consider how far the moving picture has come."

"Me . . . me in a moving picture," Miranda said dreamily, and Jerry chuckled, "Can she act! Look at that face."

"Oh, do you really think I can?" she said. "What do I have to do? I've never done any acting before unless you count the time I played Illinois in the pageant of Our Great States but I was only in the third grade so I guess that really doesn't count, but me and my friends are always acting out stor—"

"Back, back!" C.J. put up his hands as if to ward off a blow. "We'll just let enthusiasm take the place of experience."

"What part do I play?" Miranda asked.

"Jeez, you catch on fast," Bobby snickered out of the side of his mouth.

"I can pick 'em, eh, Donnelly?" C.J. said delightedly. He nudged Jerry, then turned his attention to Miranda. "Let us be serious for a minute. You watched us on Saturday. Do you think you can do exactly what I tell you to do—when I tell you—and repeat the actions endlessly, if need be? And I make no concessions for youth; every player in my Company carries their own weight. This is a blasted sight more than fun and games to us, my girl, so think before you answer."

Miranda felt dizzy, but she sat very still and put what she hoped

was a mature expression on her face. "I will try, Boss, as hard as I can. I want to be in your picture very, very, very much," she said emphatically.

"More than that I cannot ask," said C.J., raising his chipped coffee cup. "And in years to come, when the newspapers ask you how you came to the moving picture game—why, you can just say you fell into it! A toast to Miranda Gaines, newest member of The American Moving Picture Company," and he drained his cup in one gulp.

"Now," he said, "a quick smoke, then it's off to work. 'Too much rest is rust,' as the poet says." He stuck a Sweet Caporal in his mouth, then took a kitchen match from the jar on the table, and struck it on his thigh. The flame spurted to life, leaving a streak of sulfur down the tan whipcord. Absently, he slid the baseball card out of the packet, and was about to crumple it in his fist when Bobby dived for it. "Hey!" the boy cried, "I'm collectin' those!"

"What possible use could a picture of some pigskin-tossing pinhead be to anyone?" the director said.

Knowing from experience that correction was pointless, Bobby simply tucked the card in his shirt pocket and said, "You'd collect 'em soon enough if they were pictures of actresses."

"I'd rather collect the real thing," C.J. said airily.

The doorbell rang. Miranda paled—surely Auntie was busy with Jenny's wedding dress?

"Oh, Lor'," C.J. groaned. "The Widow." He grabbed Jerry's muscled arm with the desperation of a shipwreck victim clutching debris. "Do me a favor, will you? Go head 'er off at the pass. Tell her I'm not here. Tell her I'm dead, for all I care. She's got to be told we've added to the cast, and I'm in no mood for one of her tirades." He drew his mouth down, and rasped, "Misss-ter Tourneur, how dare you usurp my daughter's place . . . bleah!"

Jerry laughed and continued to drink his coffee; C.J. closed his eyes in suffering and smoked furiously.

"Why would Mrs. McGill think that?" Miranda whispered to Bobby. "I don't even know what I'm supposed to do yet."

"Doesn't matter," he whispered back. "She thinks anyone who shares the frame with Dulcie's trouble. She barely tolerates me. Dulcie's swell, though. She won't care."

Footsteps sounded in the hall and Mrs. McGill appeared in the doorway, an impressive mountain of black silk and jet beading. C.J. raised one eyebrow and blew smoke rings at the ceiling, in an attempt to appear devil-may-care.

"Why aren't you people working?" said the woman. "We do not get up at the crack of dawn to take two streetcars and the ferry to watch you all eat." Dulcie peeked around her mother's corseted waist and made a face, crossing her eyes and puffing out her cheeks.

"Madame, please," C.J. said. "I would not dream of wasting your time, nor that of your charming and talented offspring."

"Besides," Jerry added, "we can't shoot real early on account o' the shadows. Powerful tough to match the shots."

C.J. glanced gratefully at him and said, "We were having a story conference. Miss Gaines here has graciously consented to be a part of our enterprise and we were discussing her role."

"*What role!*" the woman thundered, hands on hips. "My daughter is the star of this picture and if you think I'm—"

"Madame!" C.J. snapped. "I am acutely aware of your daughter's importance to this film, perhaps more so than you." He waved the cigarette, scattering ashes across his plate. "I give you my assurance nothing will jeopardize her status."

If that Mrs. McGill wasn't a picture person, thought Miranda, I'd just bet she'd get along fine with Old Lady Duncan.

"I trust Mr. Tourneur, Mamma," Dulcie said, "and I'm glad Miranda's going to work with us. What part is she going to play, Charlie?"

"I haven't explained it to her fully, My Pet, but she is to play your little sister."

"Oh, goody!" cried Dulcie, clapping her hands. "I never had a

little sister." She darted across the kitchen and hugged the startled girl. "Isn't this going to be fun?"

"Good girl, Dulcie," Bobby murmured approvingly. "As if on cue."

"Yes, yes," said C.J., "bags of fun." He ground the cigarette into a half-eaten piece of toast and stood. "Shoo, shoo, my little chickens," he said, flapping his hands at them. "Off to the salt mines."

"Can I help with the washing up, Mrs. Donnelly?" Miranda asked as the room emptied.

"Bless you, what a sweet thing you are. And please call me Mary like the rest of 'em," she answered. "No, dearie, you run along with the others now. I'll be over in a bit with your costume."

Oh, golly, thought Miranda. I get my very own costume. Maybe a ruffly dress like Dulcie's. Maybe a gown with a train or a swirly cape. Something elegant, I hope.

She opened the screen door and stood on the back stoop. The Company was strolling along, chattering companionably as they walked beside the fence bordering the old garden. Jerry came around from the front of the house and joined them; he had gone upstairs to get Baby from his makeshift laboratory. The camera rested easily on his shoulder as he strode along conferring with C.J. Bobby and Dulcie walked with their heads together, giggling about something. Mrs. McGill followed close behind.

"Oh, no," Miranda whispered. They *would* use the street door, she thought, and what excuse could I give them for going 'round back? I'll have to take my chances.

She waited until they were all in the lot and the door shut behind them, cutting off Bobby's "Come on, Red, hurry up," then sidled along the fence until she reached the sidewalk. She stared across the street at the Duncan house, searching for signs of activity, but all appeared quiet. She watched the second-floor windows until she was positive no binoculars poked between the drawn curtains, then dashed to the door. She lifted the rusty latch, slid through sideways, and slammed the door with a resounding bang.

"Whew!" she gasped—and stopped. Bobby was leaning against a tree a few feet in front of her, arms folded.

"Why the jackrabbit dash, Red?" he said coolly.

"I—I was practicing being an actress," she said, "pretending someone was chasing me." She ducked her head and ran past him to where Jerry was setting up the camera. He stared after her, a puzzled expression on his thin face.

A-a-a-and Action!

Jerry had parked Baby in front of the shed again, this time about twenty feet from the steps, and was signaling with both arms while he squinted through the camera. Georgie walked back and forth in front of him, his forehead knotted with concentration.

"Over . . . over to the left," Jerry said, waving a hand to one side. "No, your left, not my left. My left would be your right. Go toward the fence three steps. Stop. Got 'er!"

Georgie fished a rough wooden spike out of his back pocket and rammed it into the ground, tamping it in with his boot heel. They repeated the procedure until four spikes outlined a square in front of the shed, then Georgie tied string from spike to spike. The line just cleared the grass.

"What's that for, Mr. Donnelly?" Miranda asked.

"I'll show ya. Have a look-see through that."

Miranda stretched up onto her toes and peered through the side of the camera. She could see the grass and the front porch and, immediately beyond the corners of the frame marked on the lens, the twine square.

"We was markin' off the camera range," Jerry said behind her. "You can move where y' want and as long as y' stay inside the line yer in the frame. See?"

"Ah, Donnelly," C.J. said as he strolled toward them, "trying to turn my new actress into a camera jockey?"

"Never hurts to learn all y' can." Jerry laughed.

C.J. crooked a finger at Miranda, and she trotted over to him. "Now, Miss Miranda, let me explain what I want you to do. We shall begin today's shoot with you lying in the grass. Then, you will—" and he bent down and whispered in her ear.

Jerry opened a door on the camera to check if the painstakingly measured loops of film were even, locked down the gate, and snapped the door shut. Bobby came up beside him and waited.

"Jer'," he said, "can I talk to you for a minute?"

"Sure, as long as y' don't interrupt me routine. Gotta be ready to roll when His Nibs gives the word."

Bobby stuck his hands in his pockets and traced a circle on the ground with his foot. "Maybe I'm making too much outta this, but—oh, I don't know. . . ."

Jerry reopened the camera—the film was lying snugly against the satin-covered pressure pad—clicked the door shut, and said, "Stop chewin' on it and spit it out."

Bobby frowned at his circling foot. "Have you noticed there's something funny about that kid?"

Jerry took his head out of the camera and looked at the boy. "Who, Mirandy? I don't know as how I'd be callin' her funny. A bit high-strung maybe."

"Nah, Jerry, that's not what I mean." He lowered his voice. "She's always sneakin' around, has been since the day we moved in. And did you see her when the doorbell rang? She jumped like a scared rabbit. Just now I caught her running through the door back here like, like—she acts half the time like she's got a price on her head."

Jerry took a bottle of alcohol and a wad of cotton wool from the

box next to the tripod, and began to wipe down the lens. "Maybe she's just skittish, lad. 'Member the first time you was in front of the camera? Ran behind the set and lost yer lunch, y' did. Talk about a scared rabbit!"

"Aw, be fair," Bobby said. "It's not like I don't like her—I like her fine—but what's she up to? You know she lives right next door."

"And how would y' be knowin' that?"

"I saw her. Why's she come and go through the woods when she could just walk across the yard? I tell ya—"

Jerry patted Bobby on the shoulder. "Now, Robbie, you stop bein' so suspicious-like. You know yer not much o' one for trustin' folks." He felt the boy's shoulder stiffen under his hand, but he went on:

"You heard what she said, 'bout her folks bein' dead 'n' all. If it's bad for her at home—well, that's more'n enough to make anyone a mite peculiar. You should know that, Robbie." Bobby tightened his mouth and stared at the ground. "Maybe she's embarrassed 'cause we wouldn't be welcome there. Did y' think o' that? No, I can see not. Could be she don't like folks pryin' into her life any more'n you do into yers." He saw the pained expression on Bobby's face and thought, Oh Jesus-Mary-'n'-Joseph, Donnelly, y' gone too far.

"Don't go buyin' trouble, lad," he said kindly. "We got our fair share already. Keep mum, eh?"

"Okay, Jer'," Bobby said slowly. "I won't say anything to anyone."

The street door slammed and Mary entered, carrying a bundle of clothing and the ever-present sewing basket. "Here I am, Miranda," she called gaily. "Come and get it!" Miranda ran over to her, smiling all the way. "Just put it on over your clothes. It'll be different from the other day, but C.J. said you came down so fast who could tell what you had on, anyhow? Be sure to bring the same

shoes every day, though, so the shots'll match," and she handed a garment to the girl.

"A pinafore? That's it?" Miranda looked at the wad of faded blue cloth in her hands, then up at Mary, and tears welled into her eyes. "I'm gonna look like a big babee-ee-e-e," she wailed.

Mary knelt in front of her and took her hands. "You're playing a young girl, dearie, Miss McGill's little sister. You're almost as tall as she is, so we have to fool the eye."

C.J. strode over to them, bellowing, "Tears? On my set? Not unless the camera's rolling. 'Ere now!" this in a not very successful Cockney accent. "Wot's all this then?"

Mary frowned at him and shook her head. "I think Miranda was expecting more in the way of costuming, Charles."

"Ah-hah," he said knowingly, inspecting the bowed head and the dejected slope of her shoulders. "No velvets and plumes to make us feel like a real actress?" He took her arm and turned her around. "Hmmm. You cry rather well. I must make a note of that."

"Charles," warned Mary.

He took Miranda's chin and lifted her tear-stained face. "This is not worthy of tears. I thought I explained your role. You are The Little Sister, the little troublemaker, and you have to look like a kiddie. It's just a pinafore and a doll to carry, for pity's sake, not a ball and chain."

"A doll too?" Her despair was complete. "I could just die."

C.J.'s mouth twitched, then he said firmly, "This is the moving picture game, not real life. The audience will not see Miranda Gaines; they will see a little girl who lives on a farm. Playing a part simply means imagining you're someone else. Can you do that?"

Miranda nodded her head up and down in C.J.'s hand. "Yes, Boss," she said in a small voice.

"Played a lot of pretend, have we?"

"Yes, sir. Last summer we did *The Three Musketeers* and I fixed

up the whole thing, costumes and lines and everything. We were going to do it at Carrie's house, only Tommy had—"

"I get the picture," he said impatiently. "A regular backyard Belasco. As fine a way as any to while away the lazy hours of childhood, but that's not why I asked. Pictures aren't theater. They're looser; closer, actually, to 'playing pretend.' We're learning stage tricks don't work—even the tiniest movement is magnified, intensified by the camera. So while you're pretending you must be natural, as natural as air." ˙

"But—" Miranda's lips trembled; nothing was turning out right. "I thought you wanted me to act."

The man looked at the little face, clouded with confusion and streaked with tears, and smiled indulgently. "It's still acting, but if you do it right it doesn't *look* like acting. Just be, Miranda. Listen to my voice and ignore the camera and be. *Be* The Little Sister."

"You mean like eavesdropping? Like we were all living there and Jerry was shooting us by accident?"

"Could not have said it better myself!" he said. "Watch Dulcinea and Robert, child. You couldn't have two better examples of moving picture technique. They have thrown off the shackles of theatrical convention to enter into the glory that is film."

"You'll do fine," Mary added encouragingly. "It's just a lot to take in all at once."

"Of course she will," C.J. said. "My instincts are superb." He paused, then said, "Down to brass tacks for a moment. Everyone in this Company gets paid differently: by the day, by the week, whatever. And we do not," he said darkly, "discuss it amongst ourselves. Now, after the picture's finished I will pay you a dollar for every day you've worked. You keep count and it'll be our little secret. I assume you can keep a secret?"

One whole dollar every day, she thought, even if I do have to wear this darned old pinafore. And can I keep secrets!—and she smiled in spite of herself.

"The sun breaks through the storm clouds at last," he said.

"That's more like it. You stick with us, and you'll be a movie in no time flat."

"A what?"

"We're all movies, child! Miss Dulcie, Mr. Gilmer, Mistress Mary here. It's slang for 'moving picture people.' A splendiferous and varied lot are we mo—"

"Misss-ter Tourneur," shrilled The Widow, her voice carrying from halfway down the lot. "When are we going to start?"

"Aaaaah!" C.J. covered his ears and winked at Miranda. "Go see Miss Dulcie, child. She'll help you put on your makeup. Chop-chop!" He watched her run over to Dulcie, who was primping before a mirror nailed up on a tree, and said reflectively, "Nice quality, that kid. Emotions right on top where I can get at 'em."

"You shouldn't tell her too much, Charles," Mary said. "You know how children talk."

"Lor', woman," he said testily, passing a hand over his head. "It's not as though she were a spy for the Trust. . . ."

"Cup your hands," Dulcie said to Miranda. "Like this." She shook a small square bottle, twisted off the cap, and poured a thin stream of liquid powder into Miranda's outstretched palms. "Shut your eyes. Now rub it all over your face. Careful, don't get it in your hair."

Yuck, thought Miranda; this is worse than when we played Indians by the river and did mud warpaint. She lowered her hands and looked into the mirror. The watery reflection showed a white Miranda, with white lips, white eyelashes, and white eyebrows.

Bobby leaned against the tree, cradling his battered makeup kit on his hip. "Banquo's Ghost, indeed," he said.

"Maybe I gave her too much," Dulcie said, head tilted. She wiped off the girl's eyebrows with a cotton rag and said, "No-o-ow, we need lips and some eye-black."

"And a big hat to pull over her face," teased Bobby.

"Mbomb-meee!" Miranda wailed.

"You can open your mouth, honey, it won't crack," said Dulcie.

"Don't want it in my mouth," Miranda said cautiously. "Tastes nasty."

"I know," Dulcie giggled. "After a while you don't notice." The bottle was returned to her fitted leather case, and she took out an enameled compact of lip rouge. "Purse your lips, like this." She leaned forward and, with great concentration, dabbed the color on Miranda's pushed-out lips with her little finger.

"Gee, Red," said Bobby. "You'll be the belle of the ball."

Miranda batted her white eyelashes at him.

"Bobby Gilmer, you get lost," said Dulcie. "Go paste on your mustache or something and let an artist work in peace." She returned the compact to its niche and took out a slender foil-wrapped stick. "Look up," she instructed, and lined under Miranda's eyes with the soft grease. "We don't need much of this for you, you have such big brown eyes."

"Thank you," Miranda said, staring into the treetops, "but I'd trade them in a minute for your curly hair."

Dulcie giggled again. "Rag curlers, goosie. Every night I wash it and wind it up, and you wouldn't believe what time I have to get up so it's dry. Mamma thinks it's the Mary Pickford road to fame and fortune. Here, spit on this," and she held out a cake of mascara. Miranda spat. Dulcie rubbed a short bristle brush around on the inky surface. She brushed the sticky black liquid onto Miranda's eyelashes, then stood back to admire her handiwork. "You look grand!"

Miranda squinted at the mirror. "Why do our lips have to be such a funny shade of red?"

"It's not for the stage, honey, it's for the camera. Anything plain red will photograph black."

Miranda was not convinced. "I look like the doll my friend Carrie's grandmother brought her from Paris."

"You'll see," said Dulcie. She looked over Miranda's shoulder into the mirror and poked at the tinselly curls framing her face. "You'll look just ducky on film."

Positions were set for the first scene of the day. Dulcie and Bobby were on the porch as before; Miranda lay in the grass in the hated pinafore. C.J. stood over her, an expectant sparkle in his eyes. "Remember what we discussed, and what I told you to do?" She nodded. "Just follow my commands, like playing Follow the Leader. Keep your eyes shut until I say otherwise—and whatever you do *don't look at the camera.*"

Miranda closed her eyes. The sun limned a swirling collage of red and yellow on the inside of her eyelids, and she could feel its warmth. She could feel every blade of grass along her bare forearms, pricking through her cotton stockings down the back of her calves to her shoe tops; she could hear Dulcie and Bobby breathing and every step of his booted feet as C.J. walked over to the camera. She could hear a bird near the fence calling plaintively on two descending notes: *kee-deee, kee-deee.* She could feel the air moving the loose wisps of hair at her temples, those fine strands that would never stay in place no matter how much she brushed or how tight she did up her braid. She could hear her heart beating and feel the exhaled breath fanning over her painted mouth. She heard C.J. clear his throat, and all of a sudden wanted nothing more than to get up and rush home and bury her head in Auntie's lap.

"Roll camera!"

What am I doing here? Miranda thought frantically. I'm not supposed to be here. I'm not even allowed to be anywhere near these people or—

"A-a-a-and action! Dulcinea, My Sweet, throw your hands up in horror. Good. Now scream. Ye gods! you'll have every dog in the neighborhood down on us. Robert, if you laugh . . . grab her arm. Grab her! Good. Now run down off the porch, you two. The poor innocent child that drives you wild may have been hurt. Miss Dulcie, a few tears at this point would be just the ticket. Well, look sad at least. Lovely, lovely, I could weep myself. Run over to Miss Miranda. Ladies first, you rude boy."

Miranda heard footsteps come closer and closer until the light

over her was blotted out. Bobby and Dulcie were panting with exertion and emotion. "Kneel down, you two. Dulcie, grab her and pillow her on your lap." Hands reached under and pulled her backward until she was propped limply against Dulcie's thighs. She felt soft fabric beneath her neck and heard the muted rustle of linen petticoats. She smelled the medicinal tang of makeup and the soapy odor of clean hair, and sweat, and eau de cologne. Violets, she thought; Auntie uses lavender.

"Untie your hat, Miss Dulcie."

"Whatever for," Dulcie said without moving her lips.

"Genius at work, you gorgeous creature, genius at work."

Miranda heard Mrs. McGill make a growling sound deep in her throat, and the soft rasp of velvet on velvet as Dulcie untied the streamers.

"Fan her," C.J. ordered. Miranda felt the hat pass over her face and the breeze from the movement. "Enough. Put it behind you in the grass."

"Now, Miss Miranda, listen to me. Open your eyes ve-e-e-ry slowly. Fine. Look around. Don't move your head—move your eyes. Good. Dulcie, stroke the little darling's fevered brow. Look up at your sister, Miss Miranda; give me bewilderment, confusion. Ooooooh," he sighed in a syrupy falsetto, "where am I? Where am I? Good! Now try to sit up, and you, Dulcie, force her back down on your lap. It's too soon—she may pass out, the little nuisance."

Miranda looked up at the two actors. Bobby's mouth was drawn into a worried frown, but his eyes looked reassuringly into hers, sending the message: "Come on, Red, you're doing fine." Dulcie had about her the glow of a Renaissance madonna. The sunlight filtered through her hair and diffused into a shimmering radiance around her head. There were tears in her eyes and a look of suffering on her face. Golly, thought Miranda, she really believes all this.

"Splendid!" enthused C.J. "Robert, start patting down Missy as if you were checking for broken bones. Go-o-o-ood, good. Lean back and cheat in, I don't want to cloak their faces."

Out of the side of his mouth away from the camera, Bobby said, "How long does he think my arms are?"

"Now her shoulders," said C.J. with relish. "Now her neck. You never know, she could've broken her precious little neck. Now feel her chin. Now put your hand up to her mouth."

"What?" Bobby muttered.

"Now, Missy, remember the plan? Do it!"

And Miranda bit him.

Bobby leapt to his feet, shaking his hand out in the air, and howled, "Ow! You little brat!" He clutched the bitten hand and wedged it between his knees, rocking back and forth. "Whadja go and do that for!"

This is it, thought Miranda. The palms of her hands were wet, as wet as the roof of her mouth was dry. She sat up, looking not at the camera or C.J., but at Bobby dancing and moaning before her. "Wait," C.J. was screaming, "wait 'til four."

Miranda smiled broadly, as wide and wicked a grin as Jamaica Jake ever mustered, and on C.J.'s count of four she stuck her tongue out at Bobby as far as it would go.

"A-a-a-and CUT!"

Just a Machine

Just a song at twilight,
When the lamps are low . . .

Lucy's clear soprano lifted over the deep lush chords. The music drifted through the open windows to the front porch, where Miranda sat in the dark humming along. And "the flickering shadows" did "softly come and go" as the trees moving against the light from the streetlamps dappled patterns up the lawn. Miranda waited until the song ended, and she heard the papery rustle that meant Lucy was riffling through her sheet music to choose the next piece, one to suit the melancholy of a summer evening.

"'M going now, Auntie," she called.

"Don't stay too late, darling," was the distracted reply.

Tonight Carrie's dollhouse, tomorrow the river again, Miranda thought. I'm gonna need some better excuses and oh, please, she better never check with Carrie.

Come on back after supper, C.J. had told her. Something about watching "the dailies" (whoever they were), and Bobby had joked about making darn sure she filled up good as he did not care to provide any more meals for her. He had calmed down with C.J.'s explanation: "Never would've been able to create that look of utter surprise any other way, deah boy." It seemed any amount of discomfort was to be endured in the quest for that Grail of Grails, the "clean take."

She walked over to the Macdougall place and, as she had that morning—had it been only that morning?—knocked on the back door. She peered through the screen. The kitchen was dim, one kerosene lamp burning fitfully in the center of the table. She knocked again and called, "It's me—Miranda. I'm here."

"Be right there." Mary entered the kitchen, carrying a lit taper set on a saucer. She opened the door and said, "Watch your step. Pardon the candle, but in this house electricity goes for more important things than keepin' a body from tripping over her own two feet. Come along, they're all upstairs."

Miranda followed her to the stairs at the front of the house. The shadows from the guttering candle climbed the walls and threw distorted fingers across the ceiling, but she could still get a sense of her surroundings. The long hallway was bare and had been scrubbed clean. Mary led her up the stairs, the uncarpeted boards creaking beneath them.

"What're they doing?" Miranda whispered. It was like a ghost story told around a campfire: the empty house, the wavering light, the fun-house shadows.

The stairs finished at a hall ringed with doors. The door on the left burst open and banged against the wall, C.J. in silhouette against the streaming light.

"Miranda!" he cried in a sepulchral voice that echoed down the stairwell. The goose bumps rose on her arms. "I have awaited your coming with ashen brow and leaden heart. Get up here!"

She ducked around Mary and climbed to the landing, her steps

slowing with apprehension. Why is he being so mysterious? she thought. Am I in trouble again?

Bobby's voice came from inside the lit room. "Oh, not Red. I can't face her, not now."

So that's it, she thought, her shoulders sagging. He's still mad at me for biting him . . . he sounds terrible.

C.J. spread his arms to block the doorway. "Aah, child," he said grimly, "it appears Robert's injuries were more grave than first presumed." She heard Bobby moan, and Jerry murmur indistinct words of comfort. C.J.'s voice dropped an octave and trembled. "O-o-o-o-oh, what a calamity. You may enter, but steel yourself against The Dreadful Sight."

"Charles," said Mary, "what are you—"

"Hush, woman," said C.J., and shoved Miranda into the room.

The room was glaringly bright, lit by an unshaded bulb hanging from the ceiling on a frayed cord. Peeling wallpaper covered three walls; the fourth, to her right, had been freshly whitewashed. A line of chairs faced the white wall. To her left, under the windows overlooking the street, was a long table covered with machinery and cans of film. Heavy black tar paper had been tacked over all the windows. Teacups littered the floor, the contents long past drinkable, the saucers choked with cigarette ends. Miranda saw none of this. She saw only Bobby.

He lay flat on the couch against the far wall. His eyes were closed and his left hand was swaddled in a bulky bloodstained bandage. Jerry was placing a damp cloth on his forehead; he whispered something to the boy, and Bobby turned his head and opened his eyes halfway, the lids drooping over dull eyes.

"Miranda?" he said weakly. "Is that you? It's so dark in here."

"Ah, lad," said Jerry in a funereal voice, "the infection must be spreadin'. Be brave, lad, be brave."

Miranda clenched her hands to her sides and tiptoed across the room. "Oh, Bobby," she whispered brokenly. "I'm sorry. I didn't

mean to bite you that hard, I swear I didn't. I . . . feel . . . just . . . awful.''

"I forgive you, Red," Bobby said limply. He reached out to her with the uninjured hand; it trembled violently, then dropped to the couch. He dragged it up to clutch the bandaged hand and moaned, "Oh, the pain, the pain.''

"I'm sorry, I'm sorry," Miranda repeated. Tears spilled over and down her cheeks and she began to sob.

Bobby turned his face to the wall. His stomach started to jump, the bandaged hand rising and falling. He was making strangled gulping noises in his throat. Jerry had buried his face in his hands and seemed to be afflicted with a similar complaint. A terrifying snort erupted through C.J.'s nose. Bobby brought his knees up to his chest and wailed, "I—oh—I—she's cryin' again.''

Miranda stopped short, one last sob stuck in her throat.

Bobby swung his legs around and sat up on the edge of the couch. "Gotcha!"

"Gotcha?" she yelled. "Gotcha for what?"

"For taking a chunk outa my hand, silly."

She turned on her heel and flung her arm straight back. "He told me to!"

C.J. stopped mid-guffaw, the glee on his face instantly replaced by the look of the little boy who has been caught, not only with one chubby fist in the cookie jar, but with crumbs around his mouth.

Mary folded her arms and tapped one foot on the floor. "I see. I suppose you all had a fine time dreaming up how to torture this poor child?"

"Mary me darlin'," soothed Jerry. "It was all in fun."

"Don't you Mary-me-darlin' me." She marched over to Bobby and snatched off the bandage. "I thought so. How could you, Jerry Donnelly—one of my best pillow slips!" Her foot clinked against something on the floor and she bent down and felt around in the dust under the couch. "Hah! The bottle of tomato catsup went

missing after supper." She straightened up and wiped her hands on her skirt. "Grown men . . . you should be ashamed of yourselves."

"I don't mind, Mary," said Miranda. "They got me good."

"Be a sport, Mar'," Bobby wheedled. "Worked, didn't it?" and he waggled the bitten hand at her.

Mary looked down at the persuasive smile, and her anger melted away. "Oh, it does my heart good. Too serious by half, you are," she said good-naturedly, and rumpled his dark curls. Bobby ducked away from her caress and pretended to tie his shoe.

"Hey, Bobby." Miranda sat down on the couch and put a hand out. "We're even, okay?"

"Even Steven," he said, and shook her hand.

"Now that we've given Missy here a good scare—a little divine retribution never hurt anyone, I always say—what say we give her a treat?" said C.J. He walked to the back of the room and stood beside the table. "Ladies and gentlemen—assuming any of you meet the requirements of said categories—will you be so good as to be seated. Mistress Mary, a thousand pardons for any offenses, and will you please get the lights?"

Mary pulled the string and the light snapped off, plunging the room into darkness. There was a rhythmic clicking from the back of the room that sounded like someone running a stick along a picket fence, and a rectangle of light sprang onto the whitewashed wall.

Miranda settled back against the cushions. Finally! Real moving pictures!

Scratchy lines and bars flicked onto the wall, followed by unsteadily drawn numbers counting backward from ten to one and the black slate with the chalked hieroglyphs—then there it was.

"Oh, it's beautiful!" she gasped.

"I knew I liked that kid," said C.J.

The crude shed had photographed solid and worn, as if generations had come and gone within its walls. The curtains in the windows worked; the absence of glass was unnoticeable. Clear strong

light surrounded the duo on the porch, and the shadowy recess behind them gave the hoped-for illusion of depth.

"You look really swell, Bobby," Miranda whispered to him. "Much older than real life."

"This is nothing, just raw footage. Hasn't been edited yet," he said gruffly, but Miranda could tell he was pleased.

The sharp images of The Boy and The Girl moved, and smiled, and mouthed endearments, living on the smooth, clean wall. The sections comprising each take ended every two or three minutes, separated by the slate. The concentrated silence was punctuated by an occasional chuckle or groan from C.J. as the footage either pleased or displeased him, and orchestrated by the relentless snicking whir of the projector.

Suddenly Dulcie's face filled the entire rectangle of light. Miranda flinched, an involuntary "Aah!" escaping her.

"Jeez, Red, don't be so jumpy," Bobby said in her ear. "It's only a close-up."

"It is?" she said, then, "I mean, of course it is . . . I knew that." She turned her head quickly, but she could sense his stare.

They were back to the porch. The shadow of the branch above Dulcie's head shook, at first gently, then with greater and greater agitation. Miranda was busy watching Dulcie's face; she kept glancing overhead.

"Hang on to your hats, boys—here comes Miss Kitty Hawk of 1914," C.J. chortled.

Miranda watched the film and then, before she really knew what she was looking at, there she was! rolling down the roof, dropping onto Bobby like a sack of meal dumped from the back of a truck, ricocheting off the porch railing, then disappearing below the bottom of the frame.

"That was me?" she said.

"As ever was," said Bobby. "Oh, look. Here's today's stuff."

Miranda stared at the wall until her eyes burned. The girl in the film looked like her, but then again, not like her at all. She had to

admit that the shapeless pinafore did make that girl look younger, frailer, and somehow defenseless. That girl's face was a cross between her own and the doll in Dulcie's mirror. It was smooth and even—no freckles showed through the coating of white—and the painted mouth was smaller and daintier than hers. The film Miranda's eyes were immense and black and seemed to fill her face. The footage ended with Bobby's surprised wardance and The Little Sister's gleeful grimace, and the wall went white. Mary stood and pulled the light on.

Miranda blinked several times, then realized she was crouched on the edge of the couch and had bitten three of her fingernails down to the nub. Quickly, she hid her hand behind her back, straightened up, and glanced at Bobby. His expression was one of immeasurable sorrow.

"Holy sufferin' cats," he said in Jerry's brogue. "You never seen a picture before."

C.J. stopped in the act of removing the take-up reel from the projector. "What's that?"

"Jeez," said Bobby, "I can't believe it. You poor kid, you been in a cave all your life?"

"No," she said sadly. "Just New Jersey."

"New Jersey?" he yelped. "Say, this's the center of the whole picture business, more'n New York City even. You should see the big studios they got up at Fort Lee, you—"

"That will do, Robert," C.J. said mildly. "Not everyone has had the benefit of your vast experience."

"I'm sorry, Red," he apologized. "I guess it's not your fault."

"We don't even have a picture show in town," said Miranda. "Leewood Heights is just . . . plain . . . nowhere."

"Indeed," said C.J. He walked across the room and sat next to her. "One of this burg's more salient and, ah, propitious features." He took her hand and patted it. "I think it's quite marvelous that your first moving picture experience contains your own screen debut. Bloody few can say that."

I'm going to cry again, thought Miranda. She looked down at C.J.'s hand over hers. "Thank you," she said, "thank you for not laughing at me or treating me like a baby."

"Oh, my Ridiculous Child," said C.J. He leaned over and said, "I promise I will never laugh at you or treat you like a baby. Unless you deserve it."

"Cross your heart?"

"Oh, all right," he laughed. "I cross my heart," and he did so with two sweeping gestures.

"Hope to die, stick a needle in your eye?"

"Lord, no! What a dismal rhyme."

"Can I ask you a question, sir?" she said.

"Boss or C.J., child," he said. "Two points for politeness, but those 'sirs' of yours make me feel as if I should be teaching Latin to snotty little boys in top hats. Ask on, MacDuff."

"How did you get Dulcie's face so big?"

Bobby snickered and poked her in the ribs. C.J. glared at him. "Called a close-up," he said to her. "Donnelly's doing. He moves Baby in, does who knows what to her lens, casts a few spells, kills a chicken at midnight. Pretty, isn't it?"

Jerry tickled Mary; she slapped his hand away and blushed. Bobby pulled a loose thread from his pants cuff and rolled it between thumb and forefinger. They had all heard the close-up speech before.

Miranda nodded. "But—people aren't that big."

"Oh-ho, so that's what's going on in that shiny head of yours." C.J. put his face directly in front of hers and said, "Look at me. What do you see?"

Miranda looked closely at the short pug nose, the generous mouth, the round blue eyes rimmed with short sandy lashes. "Well," she said doubtfully, "your eyes are kinda red."

"No, no, no," he sputtered. "Do you see my feet?"

"Of course not."

"Right," said the director. "When you look someone close in

the face you cannot see the rest of them. No arms, no legs, none of it. You see only their face—and that's what the camera does. It's just a machine, yes, but it sees what the human eye sees. Some say more. Much more. . . ."

A dreamy reverie fell across his face, and Miranda knew what he was saying was as important to him as if—why, he looked like Reverend Fielding in the middle of a sermon, or Auntie caught up in Chopin.

"It sees beyond the human eye, into the human heart," he said slowly. His voice was soft and direct, all bombast vanished. "It sees all, forgives nothing—and you cannot fool it. As it magnifies movement it magnifies emotion, into something so intense, so wrenching, that it tears at you even as it elates you. It sees hopes . . . dreams . . . the blackness and the beauty in every soul.

"Just a machine? It takes total strangers and unites them in the dark, all travelers on the same voyage. It lifts them out of their troubled lives, and eases their troubled hearts. Do you understand, Miranda? Do you?" He looked at the trusting face and smiled. "Of course you don't. You will in time. We'll see to that."

By the Banks of the Mighty Matawan

She was fearless. She was intrepid. She was Stanley, scouring steaming jungles for Livingstone. She was Sacajawea, leading Lewis and Clark through timbered wilds. She was Miranda Louise Gaines, guiding The American Moving Picture Company to the Matawan River for a day of shooting "on location."

A week had passed since her debut, a week of leaping out of bed in the morning and falling back in at night, exhausted, guilty, and happy; a week of "being" The Little Sister, stalking The Boy and The Girl with all the tenacity of a Jack London fur trapper. According to C.J., Miranda was, if not a natural-born actress, at the very least a natural-born pest.

From what she had been able to learn about the yet untitled picture—not an easy task, for each new day brought new ideas—it was a combination of *Romeo and Juliet* and the woodsy, sentimental novels of Gene Stratton Porter. The scenario was refined and reworked, camera angles and lighting were set and reset, and the last word on any decision seemed to be the invisible presence of someone C.J. referred to in hushed tones as "Mister Griffith," "D.W.," or "The Master."

Like a line of native porters threading its way across the veldt, the Company followed Miranda along the path winding through the pines. There was a festive mood to the equipment-laden procession. They were out of the confines of the lot, the sun was shining, and Mary had packed a picnic lunch.

"Will you slow down, little girl?" complained Mrs. McGill, chugging and puffing along at the end of the line.

"Yes, ma'am," Miranda said obediently, and stopped. Bobby stopped to keep from falling over her, then everyone else on down the line like so many dominoes. C.J. slid on the slick carpet of pine needles and swore violently.

"I'll thank you not to blaspheme in front of my daughter," said Mrs. McGill.

"Oh, Mamma, please," said Dulcie. "I'm nineteen years old. I've heard swearing before."

Miranda picked her way down the path, pondering this latest information as she brushed aside the overhanging branches. No one in the Company is who they are, she reflected. Bobby's playing a grownup and he's only fifteen, Dulcie's playing someone younger than him and it turns out she's older, and the other day Jerry told me C.J.'s name isn't even Tourneur, it's plain old Turner . . . and I'm the biggest liar of all.

"We're here," she called back. "This is the spot."

The path ended beside the shallows of the Matawan. Sunlight dappled through the trees lining the near bank; the far bank was deeply shadowed by a stand of ancient willows trailing a slender curtain of branches in the water, like lazy fingers dangled from a canoe. The air was ripe with rustlings and chatterings and birdsong.

C.J. strode into the clearing, flung his arms wide, and warbled, "There is, my children, nothing so rare as a day in June!"

"It's July," The Widow said flatly.

"Nothing so rare!" he cried, unbothered by Bessie or poetic truth. "Ah, Miranda, thou hast nosed out a spot unparalleled in sylvan grandeur. Not since Adam and Eve were driven from Eden has man inhabited so verdant a bower." He waded enthusiastically into the river, calling out, "The light! Those shadows! Superb!" as he squared his hands and panned around.

"The bugs. The damp," The Widow muttered. She spread her handkerchief on a rock and lowered herself onto it, grimacing all the way. Dulcie opened a large black umbrella over Bessie's head, absently soothing as she watched C.J.'s bellow and splash.

"Give us a hand, gang," said Jerry, lifting Baby from his shoulders. He took one leg of the tripod, Miranda and Bobby the other two, and they set her in the tall grass.

"Can I ask you a question?" said Miranda.

"Us?" Bobby laughed. "Sure."

"I've been wondering about this since the very first day," she said, "and I've been meaning to ask you—why does C.J. talk the way he does?"

"You mean like a director," Bobby said.

"I don't know," she said. "Do they all talk that way?"

"Some even worse." Bobby grinned and winked at Jerry, who started to laugh. "Sorry, Red, we're laughing 'cause—you know that Griffith C.J.'s always talkin' about like he was the King of England? He *sings* on the set."

"Opera," Jerry added. "Off key."

"But sometimes he—" She hesitated, then said, "One minute he's calling us 'dear boy' and 'dear girl,' and the next minute he's so sarcastic, almost as if he didn't like us very much."

"Don't take it personally," Bobby said. "He doesn't. It's just part of the game. Directors make fun of the actors, actors gripe about the director." He shrugged, and said to Jerry, "Always been that way, I guess."

"Since the Globe, lad," Jerry chuckled. "Struttin' and roarin'

and drivin' everyone to distraction with their crazy talk. A breed apart, they are. C.J.'s a true man of the thee-ay-ter and them types'll never use one word if they can use twenty."

Bobby nodded his assent. "It's like that old saying, 'A little learning is a dangerous thing.' You might say in C.J.'s case a little Shakespeare's a dangerous thing."

C.J. snuck up behind Bobby, shaking the water off his boots, and pounded him on the back. "Oh ho!" he cried. "That's rich! Say what you want about me as long as you do it with wit."

"Thanks," said Bobby. "I'll remember that."

"What're we gonna shoot here, Boss?" Miranda asked.

C.J. rubbed his hands together. "Today," he said with relish, "we are going to drown you."

"Me?"

"Nothing to worry about," said Jerry. "It'll all be done simple-like. You'll just get a mite wet."

For the first setup Miranda climbed into a tree by the riverbank, and sat on a low-hanging branch with her legs dangling above The Boy and The Girl and their picnic. C.J. set Bobby and Dulcie in place and warned, "Don't eat any of that until we wrap the scene." To Miranda he said, "You don't need to do much for this, only your feet'll show. They're not suppose to know you're there. Blissfully nibbling their egg sandwiches until you ooch out on the branch and fall into the river; we'll use a double for that shot. Ready?"

"Yes, Boss . . . Boss? How many times am I gonna fall out of trees in this picture?"

C.J. grabbed her foot and tweaked it playfully. "If something works use it 'til it works no more, I always say."

Bobby and Dulcie pantomimed a picnic lunch while Miranda swung her feet back and forth over their heads. They got it in one clean take. Jerry reset Baby, moving her closer to the tree and pointing her up at Miranda. "Now edge sideways toward the river," C.J. instructed; and she sidled along the branch until Jerry announced "Out of frame," and "Cut" was called. C.J. walked over to the tree

and reached up to her waist. She put her hands on his shoulders and he swung her easily to the ground. He turned and called, "Mistress Donnelly, are you ready?"

"Coming, Charles," she replied, and walked over to them carrying a smallish cloth dummy.

"That's the biggest doll I ever saw," said Miranda.

"It's not a doll," C.J. said shortly. "We don't have time for toys."

"Take off your pinafore and your shoes, dear," said Mary. Miranda sat down in the grass and obliged, unlacing her shoes and handing them up with a puzzled look. "Look, Miranda, see?" Mary held the head of the dummy toward her, and she saw that its wig had been braided into one long plait.

"Although I must say there have been times when the idea of dunking you has had a certain appeal," C.J. said to her, "we shall toss the dummy into the river in your place. Understand?"

"Won't it look different?" she asked.

"Not in a long shot," he assured her. "We'll pick it up with you in the river, floundering about and calling for help, and then The Boy'll come to your rescue."

She sat in the grass and watched C.J. climb the tree and throw the Miranda-like dummy into the river. They weren't all sewing dummies after all, she thought, as it arced into the water, horsehair braid flying.

Jerry finished cranking and waded out to retrieve the dummy. C.J. descended, wiped the sap on his hands down the side of his breeches, and said, "Into the river with you, my girl. Wait—Jerry, give her the pinafore."

Miranda donned the dripping garment and wrinkled her nose. Bobby stood next to her nervously cracking his knuckles.

"Now," C.J. directed, "go to the spot where the dummy landed and on 'Action' drop down so you're completely immersed, then come up thrashing around—you're about to drown, see?—and Robert'll come to your rescue."

Miranda stripped her soggy shoes off the dummy and unpicked

the laces, which had snarled themselves into knotty clumps. She laced them on, hoping the crawly feeling of wet shoes over dry feet would stop when she got wet, and headed out into the river.

"A mite wet, he says. Huh!" she grumbled with her back to the shore. What a waste, to be in the river in all her clothes—oh, how she longed to be barefoot. "How'm I supposed to look like I'm drowning when it's only up to my waist here?" she yelled over her shoulder.

"Squat!" C.J. yelled. "If that doesn't work go out farther, but not so far we can't match the shots."

Miranda reached the place where the ripples still circled from the dummy's impact and, holding her nose, waited for C.J.

"Action!" he screamed, "go!" and shoved Bobby into the water. Miranda held her breath and sat down quickly, crouching so the water covered her head. She rose as quickly, and saw that the pinafore had filled with air and ballooned over the surface. This would never do. Bent low, and thrashing her arms to churn the still brown water into foam, she moved toward the middle of the river. She felt the muddy bottom with her feet as she edged back. The bottom dropped off and she floated out, squirming and splashing and trying to look helpless.

Bobby wallowed toward her with a determined expression. He waved his arms and cried manfully, "I'll save you, little girl!" C.J. was running back and forth along the bank, screaming "Faster! Faster!" Bobby complied, struggling heroically against the water swirling around his thighs. He reached the spot where the bottom dropped away and—with a startled "Aah!"—sank.

He surfaced in front of Miranda, water pouring down his face and from his nose. The sodden mustache was peeling around the edges, the glue barely holding. He flailed his arms and kicked frantically, trying to push back toward shallower waters.

"I can't—I can't—" he gasped, and Miranda saw the panic in his eyes. She dived at him and shoved his chest, driving him shoreward.

"Good! Good!" C.J. hollered through the megaphone. "Thrash around a bit, then pick her up and carry her to land."

Bobby put an arm around her shoulders and reached down and got the other arm behind her knees. He straightened up with her in his arms—and immediately sat down as his feet slid in the riverbed ooze. A great spume of water went up, sparkling in the sun. He staggered to his feet, and they headed once more for shore. Miranda hung onto his neck and looked pathetic. He was sputtering and choking, and she could feel his arms shaking with strain as he plowed through the water.

He blundered blindly up onto the bank and unceremoniously dumped her. He dropped to his hands and knees, gulping and coughing, deep convulsive coughs that wracked his lean frame. Tears black with eye makeup streamed down his face.

"Good God, what's all this?" C.J. said with alarm, ripping off his scarf and shoving it in the boy's hand. Bobby wiped his face, shuddered, and collapsed to the ground. After a long, unnerving pause he rolled over and sat with his knees pulled up, resting his ashen face in his hands. He blew his nose on the scarf and looked up at them, disconcerted by the hovering faces.

"Should've—told you," he gasped. "Can't swim."

Before anyone could speak Miranda blurted, "Why not?"

"Spent my life—train depots—theaters," he panted. "No water there."

"Why didn't you— Don't you *ever* pull a stunt like that again," C.J. yelled. "What was I supposed to do if you drowned? Reshoot the whole bloody picture?"

"Sorry," Bobby gulped, and started coughing again. Dulcie knelt beside him and thumped him between the shoulder blades. "There's no cause to fly off the handle, Charlie," she reproved gently. "Bobby did a fine job."

"It's my fault," Miranda interposed. "I know how deep it is and I didn't tell anyone."

"I'm not Simon Legree, you two," C.J. said shortly. "He threw

me, that's all. I was expecting a simple rescue scene, not the last act of *Camille*. At any rate, all's well that you-know-what. Luncheon, I think," he said, hastily changing the subject. "Mistress Mary? Bring on those props!"

"I want to take a walk," Bobby declared after they had eaten, fully recovered from his visit to Davy Jones's attic. "How about giving us a tour of this river of yours, Red. Any takers?"

Dulcie looked regretfully at her silk hose and French-heeled shoes. "I'd better not," she said. "I barely made it down here without ruining these." She smiled over at C.J., prone in the shade with Jerry's cap over his face. "Not exactly farm footwear, are they, Charlie?"

C.J. lifted the cap and smiled back. "Illusion, My Pet, illusion." He lowered the cap and said, "If the audience wants to look at ugly people they can stay home."

"Come on." Miranda tugged Bobby's still-damp sleeve. "We can walk by the bank."

They meandered along, leaping from stone to stone by the water's edge, clambering over fallen saplings and tangles of brush, reveling in the silence of the woods and the sweet murmurings of the Matawan. They stopped to watch a knot of dragonflies skirling emerald wings over a still, mossy pool. "It's peaceful down here, isn't it," Bobby said quietly, and Miranda whispered, "Like there was no one else in the world."

After a time they rounded a bend in the river and came upon two tall willows guarding a small clearing. Bobby was ahead of Miranda; he pushed aside the drooping branches and said, "Hey, what's this? A hobo camp?" He grabbed her hand and pulled her into the open.

A large dead birch slanted drunkenly across the clearing into the reeds at the river's edge. Attached to the rotting trunk was a structure made of flattened boxes, bits of packing crates, chair backs, a broken-runged ladder, and half of an old wicker perambulator.

Two boys were sitting on the marshy ground in front of the shack. The taller of the two was smoking a damp hand-rolled cigarette, blowing smoke forcefully and coughing after each puff. The shorter boy, his chubby face so freckled it was more brown than pink, was eating a banana. The method was his own; he nibbled a line from end to end, then rotated it as if it were an ear of corn. The banana was patterned with dirty fingerprints.

Miranda froze, caught between Bobby and the two boys like a fly in amber. She swallowed hard, then jerked her hand free.

Tommy Stowing placed the cigarette on the milk crate that served as dining room, library, and gaming table. "Hey, M'randa!" he said robustly. "Didja come to see the fort?"

Miranda found her voice. "It's really keen, Tommy."

"Whozat?" Jimmy Duncan said around a mouthful of banana.

"Bobby Gilmer. Who're you?"

"That's Jimmy Duncan and he's Tommy Stowing," Miranda said hoarsely. "They—they live down the block."

Tommy glared balefully at Bobby. "I saw that guy before." He looked accusingly at Miranda and said, "He's one of those flickers people we're s'posed to stay away from. Boy, M'randa, you're gonna get it."

"Be a pal, Tommy," she pleaded. "Don't tell on me, please. I won't tell on you."

"What'm I doin'? Your aunt finds out she's gonna tan your hide."

"Oh, yeah?" Miranda glared at him, arms akimbo, and said, "I s'pose you're allowed to smoke all of a sudden." She spotted a stack of dog-eared newspapers on the crate. "And you been swipin' your dad's *Police Gazette*s again. Hah!"

"Okay, I give," the boy said grudgingly. "Uncle. You don't tell on me, I won't tell on you."

Miranda fixed on his companion. "You too, Jimmy. You promise not to tell your mother?"

Jimmy swallowed and said, "I'm not gon' tell her nuthin'. She scares me green."

"Pact," said Miranda firmly. "Come on," she said to Bobby. "Let's go." His measured gaze went right through her. As they turned to leave Tommy said plaintively, "When you gonna come play with us, M'randa? You never play with us no more."

Oh, gosh, she thought, I have been ignoring them. All that work on the fort and I never even asked to see it. "Sunday?" she said. "After church, all day. I promise."

Not one word did Bobby say until they were halfway back to the Company, then he pulled her over to a large rock and growled, "Siddown."

They sat for a minute, listening to the river burbling past and the birds singing happily in the trees. "You are really something, Red," he said finally.

"Thank you."

"That was no compliment." His green eyes flashed angrily. "I don't know whether to throw you in the river for real, or—or never speak to you again as long as I live."

"Whatever do you mean?" she said; it was worth a bluff.

"Nice try," he said, and turned his head away as if the very sight of her disgusted him. "You don't care much what happens to people as long as you get your own way, do you?"

Miranda was silent. There was not now, and never had been, a comeback to that particular accusation.

"All that sneakin' around—I knew you were up to no good. Jerry said I should be nice to you, you were probably just skittish 'bout being in a picture for the first time." He looked at her and said coldly, "Your aunt doesn't even know you're in the picture, does she."

"No," she whispered. She clutched his arm and said, "I didn't plan on it, Bobby, not at first. We're all supposed to stay away from you 'cause you're a bad influence, show people I mean, but I had

to see what you were doing. Nothing ever happens around here and it was all so exciting." She twisted her fingers in his sleeve and said urgently, "And you were all so nice to me, and after C.J. put me in the picture I couldn't stop . . . oh, all right, I didn't want to stop. I hated lying, I did, Bobby—I swear it—but I love making the picture so much. . . ." Please, she prayed, oh please make him believe me.

Bobby sighed and said, "Oh, what're we gonna do?" and Miranda saw her chance. "You could help me out," she said hopefully.

"Yeah," he said bitterly. "I guess I'll have to. But, listen—" He grabbed her, pulled her around, and said fiercely, "You gotta think about what you do. Do you realize what a mess you've made? Your aunt could probably have C.J. arrested for using you without permission. Thrown in jail!" She shrank back from the piercing stare, and he tightened his grip until her arms ached. "If she takes you out of the picture now we'll have to scrap everything we've done. Reshoot it without The Little Sister, or get somebody else and reshoot it anyway—"

The words sank deep and a look of horror came over his face. He let go of her, and said, "We don't have that kind of money." He shoved his hands into his pockets and stared at the ground. "If we can't finish the picture we'll have to split up," he whispered to himself, Miranda temporarily forgotten.

"Maybe now you can figure out why C.J. yelled at me this morning," he said presently.

That, at least, she could answer: "Because he was mad at you."

"Aw, use your bean, will ya? He wasn't mad at me a bit—he was scared to death. If anything happens to any of us it's the end. The picture, the Company, everything."

"Auntie yelled at me like that once," Miranda reflected. "Tommy and I were playing aviators and he double-dared me to jump off the garage. I twisted my ankle so bad I had to stay in bed for a week with it wrapped up in arnica. I thought Auntie was gonna kill me—she ran over to the Stowings and carried me home, yelling

at me all the way. Then after the doctor said my leg wasn't broken she burst into tears."

"Kinda strenuous activity for a bedridden old woman." He looked sideways at her and said, "Another lie. She's no invalid, is she."

"No," she said unhappily. "Auntie—Aunt Lucy's wonderful. She teaches piano, and does dressmaking, too . . . sometimes I wonder if there's anything she can't do," she finished with a sigh. "I wish you could meet her, Bobby, you'd like her. She'd like you too, even if you are a movie."

"Aw, Jeez." He ran a hand through his hair and said, "I give up. Listen, I'll help you, but not 'cause you deserve it. I'm doing this for the Company. And I won't tell on ya; Jerry said I shouldn't go buyin' trouble. You know what we're shooting this afternoon? 'The Little Sister swears undying loyalty to The Boy for saving her life.' Fits, I'd say. He shook his head and said helplessly, "What'm I gonna do with you, Red. What'm I gonna do."

Fort Lee

"So what's in this durn crate?" Al muttered to Tony. "The way the old man carried on you'd think it was the Crown Jewels."

"Dunno," Tony said curtly. "Jus' do my job as long as the dough— W'*chout!*"

There was a blood-chilling scream from C.J. as the crate clipped the corner pole of the platform; they grunted up the steps and set it down. Cursing life in general (and two stagehands in particular), C.J. sprinted across the lot and vaulted one-handed onto the stage. "My kingdom for a hammer!" he shrieked.

Al shrugged and pulled his hammer from a back pocket. C.J. snatched it and pried up the lid of the long narrow crate. He pulled out handfuls of excelsior and flung them out of his way.

"One lousy bank a Cooper-Hewitts," Al whispered to Tony. "You'd think they was made a gold."

"For what they cost they might as well be," C.J. snarled. He reached down into the crate, alternately swearing and praying. "Safe and sound," he said after a tense minute. "No thanks to you two. I want these up in the barn and the lighting set by this afternoon, so get the generator running while you're at it."

"What're we using them things for if we got an open stage?" said Tony, pointing to the crate.

"Because in spite of what the ancient Egyptians thought, the Sun God can't do everything," C.J. said. "The generator, boys?"

The two men headed into the roofed-over section at the back of the platform, Al muttering, "I thought Lincoln freed the slaves," Tony replying, "Lincoln didn't work in pictures."

The Company sprawled in the shade of Angus Macdougall's apple trees and observed the Boss's latest explosion with lazy disinterest.

"How come we're not shooting this morning?" said Miranda. "Where's Dulcie and The Widow?"

"The Widow?" Jerry laughed. "So now we're usin' the lingo? Show some respect for yer elders, lass."

Bobby opened one eye. "Showing respect for The Widow would require earplugs and an Act of Congress," he said languidly.

"Dulcie's not in any scenes today," Mary explained. "She'll be back tomorrow."

C.J. sauntered over and flopped down in the grass. "Move over, Donnelly, you're hogging all the shade." He lay back with arms folded under his head and sighed a sigh of pure contentment. "As my Hibernian friend here would say, 'No harm done.' The Cooper-Hewitts are unblemished, unmarked, and unhurt."

"I thought Al and Tony's names were O'Reilly and Bellini," Miranda said.

"Aah, Miranda," C.J. said to the trees. "Your entertainment value to this jaded old showman grows with each passing day. Cooper-Hewitts are lights, lighting to enhance the interiors. One measly bank of mercury vapor tubes, and how they sputter and stink! Worse than Bessie with a bee in one of her hideous bonnets."

Miranda waited until he had finished, then said, "Why don't you just call them lights if that's what they are?"

"They're named for the folks 't makes 'em," Jerry said. "One o' them theater things; no one knows how they get started."

"Like whistling in the dressing room," Bobby said, "or not putting your hat on the bed."

"No doubt," said C.J. "But save the History of the Theater lecture for a rainy day. I've an errand for you and Donnelly and The Biter."

"First I've heard of it," Bobby said, and rolled over onto his stomach.

"My idea, lad," said Jerry. "Called a pal at Pinnacle. He's gonna slip me some juice out the back door. Developer, Miranda, chemicals for developin' the film. Me an' him worked together on me first job, at the old Tannhauser Studio up in New Rochelle."

"Gee, Jer'," Bobby said, sitting up. "Isn't that the one that burned down?"

"To be sure," he answered. "Made a fine picture from it, too. 'Grab yer cameras, men!' the boss yelled, and we got it all. Called it *When the Studio Burned Down.* Never seen anythin' like it in all me born days. Nothin' goes up quicker'n raw stock. Especially," (he glared at C.J.) "if y' smoke 'round the stuff."

"I distinctly saw you light your pipe in the lab the other day," C.J. countered. "Oh, get going, you three."

Jerry stood and helped Mary to her feet. "Want to come, darlin'? Been ages since we went motorin'."

"Not today, dear," she said. "I've the marketing to do. Not that I'm looking forward to it, mind. That woman in the grocer's was so rude I'm not anxious to go back."

"Oh, her," said Miranda.

"You must know who I mean," Mary said.

"It was probably Mrs. Duncan," Miranda said carefully. "Mr. Duncan owns the store and—well, people say the only reason Mrs. Duncan works there is so she can find out how much everybody in town owes her husband. So she can lord it over them, I think."

"Didn't know The Widow had kinfolk 'round heah," C.J. said in his best riverboat gambler voice.

"That's what I thought, too," said Miranda. "They could just about be sisters. Only . . . Mary? Please, pretty please, don't tell her you know me. She hates me, she really does. And she thinks show people are tra—well, she doesn't like anybody much. She'd go bothering my aunt about me knowing you, and—and the doctor said she needs complete bed rest." She felt Bobby poke her with his foot.

"Your name won't cross my lips," Mary said, patting the girl's cheek. "The less I have to speak to that woman the better."

"I do adoah these discussions of local mores and customs," drawled C.J. "But tempus is a-fugitin', y'all."

"On me blessed Mother, what did I ever do in a former life," Jerry said, rolling his eyes. "Come on, gang." He flung an arm around Bobby's shoulders and marched him in lockstep toward the street entrance, calling back, "Hurry up, Missy."

"In a minute, I've got a stone in my shoe." She dawdled over emptying an empty shoe; when the street was clear she would make a run for it. She still had to watch her step, but, as predicted, Emma had wearied of the view from her window. According to Lucy's disclosure the night before, Emma had decided she could do more damage behind the counter of the Emporium. "Making change and insinuations," Lucy had remarked under her breath.

"What's that for?" Bobby said, as Miranda walked up the drive to the car. "That's Dulcie's hat from the picture."

"Mary said I could borrow it," she said defiantly. "So I don't get freckles."

"Too late for that!" he crowed. "Oh, I get it. So you don't get caught, you mean. Some disguise. Hat's bigger'n you are. Get in . . . you can sit by the window," he added graciously.

Jerry turned the crank on the front of C.J.'s Model T Ford. The engine sputtered and coughed and wheezed; clots of oily brown smoke spurted from beneath the hood. The explosions quickened

and the engine caught with a terrifying roar. Jerry ran around and jumped in. "We're off!" he shouted over the din.

"This is some noisy motorcar," Miranda yelled to Bobby.

"C.J. says it came over on the Ark," he yelled back.

At the outskirts of town they turned north onto the road paralleling the Hudson River for the ten-mile trip to Fort Lee. There was no traffic and they had the smooth dusty stretch to themselves. Streetcar tracks ran down the center of the road; they passed the streetcar once, and the conductor waved and rang the bell. Jerry squeezed the bulb horn mounted on the door. *"Ah-ooo-gah! Ah-ooo-gah!"* the horn blatted, and Miranda and Bobby hollered and waved. Jerry threw his head back, slung one elbow out the window, and launched into "I'll Take You Home Again, Kathleen" in a lusty baritone that compensated for its lack of finesse with volume. They sang along, la-la-ing when they didn't know the words, pushing up to the last note with a joyous squeal.

Miranda untied Dulcie's hat and tossed it into the backseat. They were well past town and she could let the wind blow through her hair. "This is the life, eh, gang?" Jerry said as he urged the car up to a peppy twenty-five miles per hour. Miranda watched the telephone poles flick overhead, and thought she had never been as happy in all her life. "You bet, Jerry, you bet!"

After a few miles Jerry said, "There's a grand spot up here," and pulled the car over to the side of the road. "Let's stretch our legs. Got somethin' to show yez." They followed him through the brush and creeper vines down a narrow track. Halfway down the path he told them to close their eyes, and took their hands and led them along. When he stopped he turned them so they faced east and said, "Here we are. Open 'em."

They were on a flat slab of rock extending to the edge of the bluffs, and could see the Hudson from shore to shore. Directly ahead lay the tip of Manhattan, crowded with the stolid cream and gray buildings of the financial district. Beyond, to the south—oh! how it took the breath away.

The entire harbor spread under the noon sun, gleaming and winking and glittering like a sheet of hammered silver. Great grim ships laden with the riches of the earth and the riches of the world steamed slowly across the shining water, making for berths on the Jersey side; elegantly towering ships moved into the row upon row of docks up the West Side, the decks crowded with passengers savoring the day and the summer and the richness spread around them like a Persian carpet, calling out to friends and leaning over the railings to watch the fat red tugs nudge the liners home.

"There isn't a better city anywhere," Bobby said simply.

"Look over to the right, out in the Bay," Jerry said behind them. "See over there near the Lady? All them ugly red buildings with the towers, on that little island there?"

"What is that place, Jerry?" Miranda asked.

"Ellis Island. Immigration station, it is. Came through there five years back, I did, scared and sicker'n I ever want to be again from two weeks in the bottom of that ship. Steerage, they call it. Hell's more like. All I had in this world in me pockets 'n' on me back." He shaded his eyes with his hand and looked out at the sooty brick buildings, crowded to the shores of the scrap of land. "Tell you what I like about this country," he said soberly, "and the picture game, too, when it comes to it. There's nobody tellin' Jerry Donnelly he can't be what he wants." And he added in a husky whisper, "Not by all that's holy."

Back in the car they were silent; Jerry noticed the subdued faces and started to sing again. By the time they reached Fort Lee the delicious sense of playing truant had returned, and spirits soared treetop high.

"If this is the center of the whole picture business," said Miranda, "then how come it looks like any old town?"

"The studios aren't out in the open," Jerry explained, "but they're all over these parts. Pinnacle is out from town a ways."

They crossed Main Street, where the spur for the trolley down to the Manhattan ferry joined the main line; four blocks beyond

the junction they turned onto a wooded road and drove west, away from the Palisades. After two miles they came upon the village of Coytesville, one unremarkable block centered around a two-story frame building with a wooden porch and a steeply pitched roof; the sign on the porch roof identified it as Rambo's Hotel. As they drove past, Miranda looked down the block and saw a man, bareheaded and in shirtsleeves, fling open the front door of the hotel and stagger out onto the porch.

What happened next took no more than fifteen seconds. Before the door swung back, a second man stepped through and pulled a revolver from his belt. There was a sharp *crack!* and smoke wisped up from the barrel. The first man lurched into the dusty street and fell. He writhed convulsively for a few seconds, kicked once, and was still.

"Jerry, stop!" Miranda screamed. "Stop the car!" She fell across Bobby and grabbed his arm, and he stomped on the brake pedal. The rear of the car slewed into the weeds at the side of the road. Jerry shifted into neutral, laid his forehead on the steering wheel, and groaned, "What is with you, Mirandy?"

"Yeah, what's the big idea?" Bobby said, his voice shaking. "I just went deaf in this ear."

"He shot him," she whispered. "At the hotel. He shot him."

Jerry looked back, and burst out laughing. "Take another look-see, darlin'."

Miranda opened her door, stood on the running board, and looked across the top of the car. The man in the street got up and brushed off his pants, assisted by his assailant. "Look across the street," Jerry said. "See? By the stable?"

"Oh," said Miranda. "A camera. Like Baby." She got back in the car, shut the door, and folded her hands in her lap. "I'm sorry, Jerry. I feel like—"

"Like a big dope?" Bobby grinned. "Poor Red. Thought you'd seen your first murder."

I guess this really is the center of the picture business, she thought. It's just moving pictures all over.

After negotiating another two miles of winding dirt roads, they reached what looked to Miranda like the picture of the factory in her Civics book. The entrance, wide iron gates in a chain-link fence, was guarded by two men in rough clothing carrying shotguns. They were both taller and heavier than Jerry—and they looked about as welcoming as The Widow.

Jerry stopped the car in front of the gates. One of the burly men came over and growled into the window, "Who're you and whaddaya want?" Before Jerry could answer he leaned down and said, "Donnelly? Jerry Donnelly, is that you?"

"Bert McGraw!" Jerry cried. "Well I'll be. Didn't know y' with that peach fuzz."

The man fingered his shaggy handlebar mustache, laughed, and said, "Ain't seen you in donkey's years. Heard you traded a shotgun for a camera. Wasn't you over at the Biograph for a spell?"

" 'Bout three years," Jerry said. "Left coupla months ago. Hitched up with C.J. Tourneur when he started The American."

"That one?" Bert chuckled. "Piece of work, he is. I hear tell he's an okay director, though."

"I'll say he is," blurted Miranda. "He's the best."

"Spoken from her years of experience," said Bobby. Bert laughed again, and Jerry introduced them to the guard. "These two're actors, Bert. Right now we're shootin' a real darlin' feature, a five-reeler. Gonna put us on the map."

Bert stuck his head into the car and said in a low voice, "Can I talk free?" and glanced at Bobby and Miranda. "Go on," said Jerry. "They're harmless, them two."

"Be careful, will ya, Donnelly? That Laemmle fellow's hauled the Trust into court again, but they're still pullin' their old tricks."

"McCoy," Jerry said, and his hands tightened on the wheel.

"None other," Bert said sourly. "Him and his trained baboons.

That's why we doubled up on the guard."

"That's why we parked ourselves in the middle of nowhere," said Jerry. "We're not takin' no chances, neither."

Bert fished around in his pockets and found a pencil stub and the lid to a box of matches. "Here. Gimme the number where you are—you do got a phone, doncha?—and I'll keep my ear to the ground for ya."

Jerry scribbled the number, handed the paper and pencil through the window, and said, "Thanks, Bert. Yer a true pal."

"Jes' keep your nose clean," said the man. He swung open the gates, and waved them onto the premises of Pinnacle Productions.

They drove up the lane and parked in the shadow of a long one-story building marked "Laboratory." Jerry got his cap from the backseat and said, "Why don't you have a good poke around?" He walked up the steps on the side of the building and went inside.

Bobby pushed Miranda out of the car and stood behind her on the running board. "What do you want to see first, Red?" His voice trailed off and Miranda followed his eyes. The building next to the laboratory was over three stories high; the looming walls were made of hundreds—thousands!—of glass panes flashing in the sun. The door fronting the grassy area between the two buildings burst open and a flood of girls poured out. Bobby's eyes widened and he jumped off the running board.

"Are those showgirls, Bobby? Like from *The Follies*?"

"You betcha!" he said, combing his windblown hair with his fingers and hastily tucking in his shirttail.

The group came toward them, chattering and laughing. Their filmy frocks were laden with lace and frippery; their wide sheer hats were lavished with silk flowers and fluttering ribbons. One tiny vivacious girl was a prairie flower amid a rose garden. She was costumed as a cowgirl, from the ten-gallon hat perched impertinently on her dark curls to the gun belt slung over her divided skirt. The girls giggled their merry way along, trilling hello's as they passed.

When they had rounded the corner of the building, Bobby sighed and said, "Bet they came from the shooting stages. Let's go see."

A long green touring car purred by and pulled up in front of the glass building. A chauffeur in matching livery got out of the open front, circled the car, and opened the rear door. A stately woman in trailing emerald velvet emerged and swept into the building, dragging long furs through the dust.

"Is she a star?" Miranda breathed.

"My guess is an idiot," he snorted. "All that fur in July?"

"You have no sense of style," she said haughtily. They walked over to the open door and looked in, squinting until their eyes adjusted to the change in light.

"How many sets do you see?" Miranda asked.

"Jeez, thirty or more. Look, that one revolves." As they watched, a drawing room with the Paris skyline in the windows was rotated until the light streaming in caught it square mid-floor, and the men shifting the set strolled off behind the painted walls.

"How come we don't have glass walls?" Miranda asked.

"You're a smart kid, Red," Bobby said, eyes on the vast ceiling. "You figure it out."

She looked at the ranks of lights flanking each set, and thought of "one measly bank of Cooper-Hewitts," as cared for as new-laid eggs; she looked at the dozens of bustling stagehands, and thought of Al and Tony, who, despite their complaints, did the work of twenty; she thought of the girls they had seen, so casual and confident in their finery, and saw Mary sitting in the shadow of the fence, mending what were little more than rags. She looked around at the myriad sets and the transparent walls rising to the sun, and thought of a single row of cubicles in what had once been a garden.

"It's about what you said the other day," she said slowly, watching Bobby's face. "Why it's so important that nothing go wrong. There really isn't much money for the Company, is there?"

"No, there is not," he said gravely. "It's not that bad, though. All this fancy gear doesn't mean they're making better pictures'n

we are. C.J. always says it takes more than money to make a good picture. He says talent and energy—real vision—beat money in the long run." One corner of his mouth lifted and he said, "Of course he usually talks like that when the money's rollin' in."

"Bobby, what's the Trust?"

"So you did catch that," he said sharply. "You ever heard of Thomas Edison?"

"We learned all about him in school. In third grade," she said witheringly. "He's a great inventor, you know."

"Pardon me, Madame," he said, and bowed to her. "No, Red, I'm tellin' ya—he may be a great inventor, but I'd like to sock that guy right in the nose."

"For Pete's sake, why?" she said in a shocked voice.

Bobby leaned a shoulder on the doorjamb and looked out over the stages. "Says he invented the moving picture camera. Maybe he did, but he didn't patent it quick enough. Never thought it'd amount to more'n a toy, C.J. says. Anyway, people start makin' pictures, and they start makin' money. So Edison gets sore and patents the only thing left, the sprocket holes."

"But what difference would that make?" she said. "I know what those are. Jerry showed me. They're just those little holes on the sides of the film."

"It's the most devious thing he coulda done." He turned and rested his back on the doorjamb. "They hold the film in place, see? You can't run a camera without 'em," he explained. "They tried to get around it at the Biograph—you know, where we all used to work, where we all met? They cooked up this camera that punched the holes as it went along. Jerry says the thing made more noise than a threshing machine and sprayed film doodads like mad. Everything they tried made more problems, so what they did was go back to using regular equipment—only now they had to hide it."

"Hide it from Thomas Edison?" said Miranda.

"Not him exactly. What he did was, he got together with his

cronies at the big picture companies and they formed the Trust, The Motion Picture Patents Trust. If you use patented stuff you're supposed to pay all kinds of fees, and if you don't pay up, or use foreign equipment, they can come in and shut you down." He snapped his fingers. "Like that."

"But that's not fair," she said.

"I'll say! Me, I think the patents are an excuse, like—what's the phrase? 'A means to an end.' My guess is the Trust wants people like us out so they can have the picture game all to themselves." He stared off into the studio again and said, "The stinkers."

Miranda tugged his sleeve to get his attention. "Who's that McCoy Jerry and Bert were talking about?"

"You don't suppose old Tom's gonna get his hands dirty, do you? Naw, the Trust hired every goon on the East Coast to spy on the independents. McCoy's the worst. If he scares guys like Jerry and Bert. . . . He travels with a couple of plug-uglies he got from this big detective agency called Pinkerton's; wrecking companies, smashing cameras, people, anything in his way."

"Then that's why they have the gates, and the guns," said Miranda. "To keep out the goons."

"Listen, that's how Jerry got into the picture game. He used to be a security guard like Bert, then he got interested in the cameras. You know he saved two whole years to buy Baby and all his equipment? Baby's a Pathé, too; that's why he's so protective. She's French, see? Strictly illegal as far as the Trust is concerned."

"So that's why you're in Leewood Heights," Miranda said. "You're hiding from the Trust. And I thought I had secrets!"

"Everyone's got secrets," he said, "and this one's a darn sight bigger'n yours. Just one more reason why you shouldn't make trouble. Besides," he grinned wickedly, "I got the goods on y—"

"Hey! You kids, hey!" Bert McGraw was running toward them up the lane from the gates, running so hard dust went up with every step. His shotgun was open and crooked over his arm, and he was attempting to load a cartridge of buckshot as he ran. The ammu-

nition dropped in, and he snapped the gun shut as he reached them.

"We weren't doing anything, honest," Miranda said, eyeing the blue steel barrel inches from her stomach.

"Where's Donnelly?" Bert shouted at them. "Where'd he go?"

"In the labor—" Bobby said. Bert wheeled around and headed for the low building. "We gotta find him," he yelled. "Now!"

Miranda and Bobby ran after him; Bobby caught up to Bert in front of the laboratory steps, grabbed the guard's arm, and panted, "What's up—what—what."

"I got a man at the docks," Bert bawled. "McCoy's on the noon ferry. Spot inspection, he said, and you know what that means."

Bobby thought fast. "I'll get Jerry—you go—"

"I'm ahead a ya, kid. Just get outta here, fast as ya can!" He gave Bobby a shove up the stairs and pounded away toward the shooting stages. He ran through the open door bellowing, "Raid! It's a raid!" Men laden with boxes and bundles started running out of the wide door and in the direction of the woods. Miranda saw one man carrying a camera over his shoulder, the open tripod flapping wildly. The grand lady of the green velvet streaked through the door, Merry Widow hat over one eye and furs flying, and leapt into the back of her car. She screamed into the speaking tube; the chauffeur awoke with a start, and seconds later the car roared past in a choking billow of exhaust.

Bobby stopped at the top of the steps with one hand on the doorknob, and called down, "Start the car!"

"I can't, I can't, I don't know how!"

"It's in neutral," he yelled. "Pull out the choke—it's a knob under the steering wheel, it's marked—pull it out. The crank's under the seat—stick it in and crank. Clockwise," and he dashed through the door.

Miranda ran over to the Model T, breathlessly repeating: "Pull out the choke—crank under the seat—clockwise—" She opened the door on the driver's side, reached under the seat and found the crank, dashed to the front of the car, skidded to a stop and yelped

"Choke!" and ran back around the car. There it was, thank heavens, clearly labeled. She yanked it out, and ran back to the front of the car.

Where did you put in the crank? He bent over, she thought, so it must be somewhere down here—victory! She shoved the long end of the metal rod into the opening above the rusty bumper and turned it as hard as she could. It moved two inches—and stuck. She shook her hair out of her eyes impatiently and turned it again. Nothing. She put her full weight behind it, jumping off the ground and coming down hard. Another inch.

Behind her the air resounded with banging doors and shouted commands; the ground shook under hundreds of scurrying feet; a car lurched past, gears grinding, men on the running boards. Miranda's breath was dry in her throat, and suddenly she felt like crying. She pressed her lips together, braced her legs, and grabbed the crank; her hands were sweaty, and slipped off. "Oh, please, Mama, please," she sobbed, and clutched the crank once more.

"Honey, I don't think that's gonna work, all that jumpin' aroun'," said a voice with a sweet Southern lilt to it. Miranda turned and looked up; the cowgirl was standing over her with a bright, dimpled smile. "Lemme give y'a hand." The actress bent down and grabbed the crank with Miranda, and, on the count of three, said "Push!" With a squeal, the crank went over the top and down the other side of the circle. They pulled it up and pushed it over, and over and up, and over and up, until the engine sprang to life with its customary thunder. The cowgirl dusted her hands together and said, "There!"

"Thank you, thank you," Miranda gasped. The girl smiled warmly at her and ran off toward the dressing rooms behind the buildings.

Jerry and Bobby came out of the laboratory, Jerry lugging two large tin cans, and ran over to the car. Jerry opened the back door, heaved the cans onto the floor, and barked, "In back. On the double."

Bobby shoved Miranda in and dived after her; Jerry glanced over the seat and said, "Heads down and keep 'em there." He backed around—the car rocked and Bobby and Miranda slid into a heap—and tore down the lane toward the gates with the accelerator pressed to the floorboards.

"You got all the luck," Bobby griped as he worked himself out from underneath her. "I shoulda made you go get Jer', then I coulda talked to that girl."

"Ouch!" she said. "You've got the boniest elbows. I wasn't talkin' to her anyway, she was helpin' me start—"

"Quiet, youse!" Jerry rapped out. "I'm tryin' to keep me mind on the road."

The gates flew past the windows, and Miranda raised up until she could see through the isinglass oval over the backseat. A long sleek Cadillac sedan with brass side lamps sped by and screeched through the gates, leaving thick yellow dust hanging in the trees. She got a vague impression of a dark sharp profile bent over the wheel and two men in back, then Bobby grabbed her blouse and yanked her down.

"I saw him," she whispered excitedly. "I saw McCoy."

"Yeah? Well, don't act so all-fired happy about it," he whispered. "Keep your fingers crossed you don't ever see him again."

Help! Murder!

"Donnelly, forget you're a decent human being and grab him hard!" C.J. yelled.

"Come on, Jer'," Bobby urged. "I may be skinny but I won't break."

Jerry sighed and pulled the bandana from his back pocket, intending to mop the sweat beading his forehead. "Not the makeup!" C.J. shrieked. "Don't smear the makeup!"

Jerry sank down on the bale of hay in the corner of the barn set and moaned, "For the love o' God, Boss, can't I go back to Baby and stop all this play-actin'?"

The three adventurers had returned from Pinnacle with the two cans of developer and an agreement to "keep mum" about their brush with The Law. Why give the Boss another excuse to display his volatile temper—and "me darlin' Mary" would only "worry herself sick." Once past Fort Lee Jerry had let them sit up, and the rest of the way home they had leaned over the front seat while he related campaign tales from the Patents Trust War; of fortunes made and lost, of cameras and careers smashed, of the escapes and escapades of the seven-year battle. Miranda had thought the stories as thrilling as any Rider Haggard novel. Jerry had sounded very upset, though, and Bobby had repeatedly cracked his knuckles and muttered, "The stinkers."

On their arrival C.J. had rubbed his hands together, cackled a few times, and conscripted Jerry for the role of The Father, the humorless patriarch of The Girl and The Little Sister. It seemed the actor hired for the part had made demands. Not only had "that overweening ham" wanted his daily stipend paid in advance, he had demanded a private dressing room and a dresser. C.J.'s response had been a torrent of invective, rising in pitch, tempo, and volume to a thundered "Begone!"—so Jerry it was.

C.J. pointed to Miranda, standing on an apple crate behind the set watching through a window, and trumpeted, "If I can turn a green, unseasoned kid into an actor, then I can turn an old hand like you into a star, by Jove!"

Jerry gazed longingly at Baby (now manned by Georgie, who had been given a battlefield promotion to cameraman-for-a-day). "I can check on me darlin' after every take?" C.J. nodded. "Then me fate is in yer hands," Jerry sighed, "and may the saints preserve 'n' protect us all."

"Right," C.J. barked. "We go again. And this time try to remember that Robert is no longer your friend, but the rotten, sneaking hound romancing your daughter. You have entered your barn to do the evening chores, and found the little toad hiding— Aaaah!" He grabbed his temples and yelled, "I've got it!"

"Touch of malaria?" Bobby inquired mildly.

"Silence!" C.J. rushed over to him and said fervently, "What if you're not *hiding*, but stealing a ladder. You've got a valise all packed, see? You're going to elope with The Girl! It's bloody brilliant," he announced to the roof. "*I'm* bloody brilliant."

Bobby grabbed C.J.'s elbow, in his dancing eyes a reflection of the director's manic gleam. They jumped up and down, caroling in tandem: "It'll work, it'll work!"

Miranda leaned dispiritedly on the cut-out window and thought, They're at it again. How're we ever gonna finish this picture if they keep changing their minds?

After a small valise had been found in the house and a ladder had been dragged up into the set, they were ready to reshoot the scene. Georgie turned his cap to the back and started cranking on command, clutching his stomach with the other hand. Baby was Mister Donnelly's pride and joy and film cost two cents a foot—this was a nerve-racking business.

Jerry advanced on the hapless Boy, hands curled over his head. "Lovely," C.J. breathed. "Superb quality of menace. Robert, duck under him, come to stage center. Turn around, Donnelly—clumsily, as though you were some big ox of a stevedore."

Jerry was sweating profusely, whether from nerves or effort it was impossible to tell. Bobby had stained the big man's mustache an evil black and combed the ends down; he looked like an angry bear as he faced The Boy.

"Snarl!" C.J. ordered. "I know you never snarled in your life; try lifting one corner of your mouth. Fine. Robert, you circle him so you're side by side. Now, Donnelly, I want you to reach back with your upstage hand, and haul off and belt The Boy in the jaw, but pull your—"

Bone met flesh with a sickening thwack—and Bobby fell to the ground.

"Punch," C.J. amended lamely and buried his face in his hands. "Pull your punch."

Jerry stared with dumb surprise at his fist, then at the unconscious boy lying in a loose sprawl on the straw-covered floor. "Robbie!" he wailed, and dropped to his knees.

C.J. ran over and knelt quickly, whipping off his scarf to fan the boy's face. Miranda fell through the window, into the stall below, and scrambled across the set on her hands and knees. Georgie had the presence of mind to cease cranking, and stood wide-eyed with his fingers in his mouth.

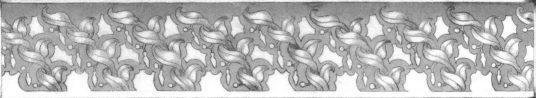

Jerry was rocking back and forth, keening monotonously: "Oh, sweet Jesus what've I done, oh sweet Jesus what've I done." C.J. stopped the useless fanning and started slapping Bobby's wrists; the discolored swelling on his jaw was already visible through the greasepaint and powder.

Bobby opened his eyes. "Thish pictursh gon' kill me," he slurred. "She bitesh me, he hitsh me . . . aw, Jer', stop blubbin'. We got the shot, di'n' we?"

"What a trouper," C.J. said with pride. "Knew what I was doing when I stole you from the Biograph prop room, deah boy."

Bobby raised up on an elbow and manipulated his jaw with a shaking hand. "Not broken," he said weakly.

"Is it always like this?" said Miranda, huddled at his feet.

"Is what always like what," said C.J.

"Making pictures . . . is it always so dangerous?"

"You wanna tell her the truth or make her feel better," Bobby said as he staggered to his feet.

"It's a tough business," C.J. said curtly. "It requires tough people. To your place, Missy. We go again as soon as Robert's got his wind."

Miranda stared through her window while the remainder of the fight between the hopelessly mismatched pair was staged and played out. "React!" C.J. screamed at her, repeatedly. "Reacting, he calls it. Huh," she muttered sullenly. "Making stupid faces is what I call it."

The long day was taking its toll. The trip to Fort Lee had been exhilarating but exhausting; she had barked her shin diving through the window; she was hot; sweat trickled between her shoulder blades; the makeup on her face had melted to a sticky smelly goo; the Cooper-Hewitts gave off a violent greenish glare that made her eyes smart. And, although she would rather have died than admit it, she was bored. After weeks of being the Company's "Little Darlin'," watching them act while she stood in the background and made faces was a blow to her newly minted ego.

Lucy would have called her cranky and overtired and sent her to bed. Without supper.

The scene ended with The Father tripping over a rake hidden in the straw, bashing his head against the corner of the stall, and sliding to his death. Jerry slumped against the wall, a carefully applied trickle of blood running down his face. (C.J. had mixed molasses and ink to get the properly gruesome effect; it worked, but the flies buzzed around the sugary glop.) While Jerry held his breath and tried to look dead, Bobby clasped his hands to his chest, his black-rimmed eyes wide with horror.

"I see you, Donnelly," screamed C.J., "sliding your eyes over at Baby. Georgie's doing fine, so look dead or I'll kill you myself. Now Robert, run toward the camera, a mad dash from the scene of the crime. Run, boy, run! as though the very Hounds of Hell were nipping your tail." The Boy fled the scene, not noticing in his panic the tell tale valise, knocked over in the straw. "Got it," said C.J. "Cut—we'll iris down on the luggage later, edit it in so they get the point. Miss Gaines, we are ready for you in front."

Bobby went to the side of the stage and got a towel from the old tin toolbox he used as a makeup kit. He peeled off his mustache and laid it carefully in the box, then rubbed the remaining shreds of spirit gum from his upper lip. Slowly, he dipped out a blob of cold cream and smeared it over his face, wincing when he reached the bruise on his jaw. Face cleaned down to the fifteen-year-old underneath, he slung the greasy towel around his neck and watched C.J. prepare Miranda for Scene 27: "The Little Sister Discovers the Body."

"Now, Miss Miranda," said C.J., "you enter the barn, stop, turn, and see your father lying dead against the wall over there. You stop again, scream and put your hands up to your face, then turn and run out of the barn, toward me, toward Baby. Have you got that?"

Miranda nodded.

"Good. The light'll start to go soon, and I don't want to run the generator for much longer, so do us all a favor and get it in one."

I'll get it, she thought. This is nothing—if I can start a car I can do this. Run into the barn, turn, stop, see Jerry. Or was it stop, turn? Oh, I'll just do it.

"Roll camera" was called, and on action she gulped, smoothed her hair off her sticky face, darted into the barn, turned toward Jerry, and stopped awkwardly.

"Cut. No, no, no," C.J. said. "First you stop, then you turn. We go again."

They went again. Miranda ran into the barn, overshot the mark where she was supposed to stop, and tripped over The Boy's valise, twisting her ankle as she went stumbling into the straw. "I'm sorry, Boss, I'm sorry."

"As Donnelly says, no harm done. Try again?"

She nodded miserably; now her ankle was throbbing.

Again she tried. Again she confused the sequence. Bobby watched dispassionately from the sidelines. Having gone to meet his maker picture-fashion, Jerry had closed his eyes for a well-earned forty winks. C.J. propped a foot on the upended megaphone and rested an elbow on the raised knee. He leaned forward and, with great patience, said, "Listen to me, child. Run in. Stop. Then turn. Concentrate."

Miranda dashed into the barn once more—and turned before she stopped.

"CUT!"

"But—" she said; then, "Why do I have to do it that way?"

C.J. put hands on hips and stared at her, eyebrows up.

"Oh, you little ninny," Bobby muttered.

"Why does it matter if I turn before I stop or stop before I turn?" she persisted. "I don't see what difference it makes."

"Pardon *moi*, Miss Bernhardt," C.J. said acidly, "I didn't realize you spoke English. You will do it that way because *I tell you to do it that way.*"

"But I can't get it right," she said stubbornly. "I don't—"

Bobby crossed the set in two long strides, grabbed her mid-sen-

tence, and said to C.J., "Let me handle this." He took her roughly by the upper arm and dragged her across the stage, down the steps, and around to the back of the platform. C.J. called out, "Five minutes and not a minute more." He lit a cigarette and muttered, "Wake up, Donnelly, you're missin' all the fun."

"Ow, Bobbee-e-e-e, you're hurting me," Miranda whined. He freed her arm, and she rubbed it and glared at him. "Why'd you do that?"

"Because, because—" He whirled around and slammed a knotted fist into the pole behind him. Miranda froze—there was a darkness beneath the smiles and the banter, and for a moment she was frightened. He kept his back to her for a minute, then turned and leaned on the pole. He scowled down at her, his black eyebrows drawn together. "You know darn well why," he panted. "I know you're only a kid, but—"

She opened her mouth and he cut her off brusquely. "You think you're some hotshot now, doncha? Gettin' away with murder these days, that's you. Cut the look—you know I'm right. Makes sense; you never been anywhere or done anything and this is all pretty heady. And don't think I'm just being a crab, 'cause that ain't it."

"Well, it was hot and I was tired and I couldn't get it right and what'd I do that was so bad anyway?" she said.

"You were acting like a big fat stuck-up actress."

"But I am an actress," she said indignantly. She looked up at the angry face; her chin quivered slightly and she said in a doubtful voice, "Aren't I?"

The scowl relaxed. "Listen," he said, "you're in the moving picture game, that's all. Say you make pictures or say you're in the picture game, but don't go calling yourself an actress yet. You're too young to start all that actressy guff; putting on airs, acting like you think you're some kind of star. I'm no star and neither are you, and don't you forget it."

"But Dulcie's an actress and she doesn't act like that."

"Aw, she wouldn't know how to throw her weight around on a

bet. Dulce's different. So'm I, for that matter. We both been kicking around the theater since we were babies. Learned a long time ago to shut our traps and do what we're told. It's called 'taking direction.' "

"O-o-oh," Miranda said slowly. "I see what you mean."

"Yeah, well, I hoped you would." He shook his head with irritation. "You think I keep yammering at you just to hear myself talk? You got enough brass to plate a doorknob, kid, and—heck, somebody's got to stop you from making a complete fool of yourself. C.J. was this far from blowing his top for real, and that's the last thing we need. And as for being hot and tired, what about me?" He fingered his jaw. "I took a roundhouse right smack on the pan and kept going. Making pictures is *work*."

She stared at the ground, cheeks burning. "I guess I've got a lot to learn," she said diffidently. "I'll try not to act like . . . oh, I could just die." *I always say that,* she thought, *but this time I mean it.*

"Aw, you weren't that bad. I just wanted to catch you before you got worse." He spat on his palm and offered his hand. "Friends?"

"You bet," Miranda said with relief. "Friends forever." She spat in her palm and they shook hands.

"Hello-o-o?" C.J. stuck his head between the muslin drapes above their heads. "What news on the Rialto? Do I get to shoot another death scene?"

"No such luck." Bobby grinned. "I'm just pounding some sense into the big star here."

"Don't pound her into the ground, boy," he said with a twinkle. "We've got to nail that scene by sundown if it kills us all."

"I'm sorry, Boss, honestly I am," said Miranda.

"Apology accepted. In every sense of the word this has been a bloody day."

"I got it straightened out, Boss," said Bobby. "She won't give us any more trouble."

"That," said C.J., closing the curtains, "remains to be seen."

Rain Delay

The rain started midmorning, mid-scene, great fat warm drops at first, the sky not perceptibly darkened. Within minutes the rain was heavy and cold, fierce slashing sheets from green skies. With the first sprinkle Jerry grabbed Baby and ran for the house, leaving the others to hurriedly cover what furniture and equipment could not be moved; all that could be moved was recklessly crammed under the platform. C.J. directed the evacuation, crisply bellowing orders with the fervor of a drill sergeant, machine-gunning commands over the rain and the wind.

Bessie scuttled for cover with her skirts up to her knees, affording all who cared to look the sight of bony legs in remarkable lilac hose. Dulcie stayed with Bobby and Miranda; still in costume, they pulled cumbersome tarpaulins over furniture and carried chairs around and down under the stage, all the while dodging the sodden drapes that snapped and swayed and groaned like the rigging of a ship breasting high seas.

By noon nothing more could be done. C.J. dismissed the crew and headed back to the house. The Boy, The Girl, and The Little

Sister ran shrieking with laughter down the deserted lot, through the dripping orchard to the street door.

Bobby jumped off the curb into the street. The rain had churned the hard-packed dirt to mud, and he wallowed along in a *grrr*-ing, snarling imitation of a dancing bear. Dulcie pirouetted around him, holding out saturated skirts in a parody of daintiness. Miranda lurched behind bent double with helpless giggles, for once not caring if Aunt Lucy or Emma Duncan or the whole town saw her.

Bobby took their hands and danced them alongside the house. They pranced through the back door, and stood giggling and shivering and dripping on the mat. He yanked their hands up, then down, pulling them into a bow. "A great performance deserves a curtain call," he gasped.

C.J. was stomping up and down the middle of the kitchen, wrapped in a old quilt that trailed on the floor. His beloved boots oozed water with every step. "Rotten wet damned East Coast," he grumped. "Money down the drain. Money down the ever-lovin' drain. By Jove, I'll take the whole shooting match out West, I will, I'll—" He pivoted at the end of the kitchen and saw them. "Oh, Lor'. Look what the proverbial feline dragged in. Too bloody bad we're not shooting *The Spoilers.*"

"We were dancing," said Dulcie. Her curls hung in clammy ropes, her eye makeup ran in smeary black rivulets down her cheeks, and the frilly muslin dress was a limp rag. Bobby and Miranda were equally wet and disheveled; all three were muddy to the knees.

"If it was a rain dance," said C.J. sourly, "you're all fired." He flung the tail of the quilt over one shoulder and strode from the room, an angry Roman senator leaving the Forum—and a trail of wet footprints.

"What do you suppose got into him?" said Dulcie.

Bobby put a finger to his lips and waited until the footsteps receded down the hall. "Don't tell your mother, but—"

"Bobby Gilmer, you know me better than that," she retorted.

"Sorry, Dulce." He pushed the hair off his forehead and said in a low voice, "I think from a coupla things I overheard the money's running short. We've been shooting more footage than Jer' planned on, and getting rained out didn't help. My guess is he's just worried."

"We are going to be able to finish the picture, aren't we?" said Dulcie.

"Sure, Dulce," he replied. "Sure thing."

The rain continued throughout the afternoon. The skies remained dark, more night than day. The wind whipped furiously, knocking the trees at the roof, strewing broken branches over the yards along the street. Jerry had driven over to the City on some mysterious errand, ignoring Mary's lamentations about taking the ferry in a storm; the McGills had gone along, glad to be spared the streetcar on such a day. C.J. had locked himself in the projection room and could be heard pacing back and forth in an endless troubled cadence. Mary was at the kitchen table snapping green beans into a bowl, her eyes red-rimmed. For once she had shooed them out of the room.

Bobby and Miranda were in the parlor in front of the fireplace. Dry clothing and a cheerfully crackling fire helped push back the darkness and the cold, but did little to dispel the tension that seemed to permeate the very walls of the house.

Miranda sat on the floor holding a wire popcorn basket near the flames. She shook the long handle and watched the kernels jump and slide, waiting for the nutty aroma to rise. Bobby sat on a stool, chin resting on his fists. The flames darted and leapt, throwing his face into light, then shadow, then light. His eyes shone dark and dreamy.

Miranda listened to the rain clicking against the windows. After a time she said, "Mary's been crying."

"Worried about Jerry in this weather, I expect."

"Her wedding ring's gone."

"Are you sure?" he said quickly.

"I'm pretty sure it was on her hand this morning," she said. "She never takes it off and now it isn't there."

"Damn," he said. "If she's popped her ring we must be down to the bone."

"What does that mean?"

He stared into the fire. "It means that Mary's crying because she gave Jerry her ring to pawn, or sell, to buy the film stock we need."

"Oh." She thought for a minute, then said, "I've got twenty-eight dollars. I could give it to C.J. if it would help."

He looked at her suspiciously. "Where'd you get that kind of money?"

"Birthday and Christmas and candy money for a year. I've been saving it."

"Whatever for?" he laughed. "You've got enough books for three people and you're always squawking on about how you're too old for dolls."

Miranda turned her head toward the fire and shook the popper. The corn was starting, a few white nuggets bouncing at the end of the basket. She sighed deeply, and in a voice burdened with tragedy said, "Run away from home."

Bobby leaned forward and stared at her. "Let me guess," he said levelly. "You were going to run away because 'Nothing ever happens in this dumb old town.' You are such a baby."

"That's not fair," she protested. "You don't know what—"

"No," he said. "You don't know. Being on your own, it ain't a bit like Huck Finn." He glared at her for a moment, then said, quickly, "You ever been hungry?"

"For Pete's sake, what kind of a question is that? Of course I've been hungry."

"I don't mean the kind of hungry when you're late for supper. I mean hunger so bad it twists inside you. Hunger so bad that stale food, or rotten food, tastes good."

She stared up at him, and shook her head.

"Well, that's what being on your own is. . . . Never knowing if you're gonna eat or not. Never knowing if you're gonna have a place to sleep, or what you're gonna do tomorrow. No home. No one who cares. You just don't understand, do you?" He clenched his fists on his thighs, the knuckles whitening, and said angrily, "You've got your aunt, and a roof over your head, and—and a clean bed to sleep in and you want to run from all that? Oh, you just don't know."

She stared back, but intuition kept her silent. There was such intolerable misery on his face that, for a moment, she wanted to avert her eyes as one would from something deeply private, or an accident.

"You just don't know," he repeated, and his voice sank to a rough whisper. "Oh, I envy you. 'Nothing ever happens'? God, how I long for a life where nothing ever happens—"

This was more unsettling than the afternoon by the river, more frightening than the day he had accused her of acting stuck-up. She had to do something—anything—to wipe that shattered, shuttered look from his face. She banged the basket down, scooted across the floor on her knees, and knelt beside him.

"Oh, Bobby, please," she begged, hands clasped under her chin. "Please don't be mad at me. We're friends, aren't we, please? How could I know? How could I? If you only ever spend your life in one place you always feel like you're missing something. It all sounded so wonderful and independent to me, what you did, I mean. Traveling around, being in the theater."

"The theater," he said bitterly, and looked over her head. "Life on tour. 'The song of the open road.' Glamour and fancy costumes and flowers on opening nights. Most people think that's what it's like, I guess."

Miranda waited, and watched the firelight play over the planes of his fine-boned face. He turned and caught sight of her eyes, so wide and dark and anxious, and smiled inwardly. When he spoke his voice was gentle and weary, as though anger was no longer worth the effort.

"I'm sorry, Red," he said. "I've got no business gettin' sore at you. It's not your fault you thought I was some kind of adventurer. I could tell you what it was like, if you really want to know."

"Yes, please," she said softly.

"Oh, Miranda. Glamour? We went from one town to the next, small towns, ugly, dirty little towns. The theaters were cold in the winter and hot in the summer and smelled like—oh, I don't know—dirt and damp and old greasepaint and sweat."

He looked off into the darkness beyond the flickering light. Miranda stayed very still, and her eyes never strayed from his.

"The hotels were as bad as the theaters . . . that is, when we could afford one and didn't have to sleep in a dressing room. I—I never went to school. Not regular, I mean. If we had a long engagement I'd get a month, maybe two. Always the new kid. Always different. You got any idea what that means?"

"Yes," she whispered.

"Yeah," he said slowly. "Maybe you do, at that. No parents and all."

"Bobby?" she said tentatively. "Who's we?"

"Me and my mother. She was an actress. Second leads, mostly. Smaller parts as she got older. Died a coupla years ago. Never knew my old man. Died before I was born, she said. Took off is my guess. . . . So what were your folks like?"

A log fell and a shower of sparks burst like a firecracker, hissing and spitting against the stones. Miranda turned and looked into the leaping flames. How could she answer? It was all fragments, like the bright quick sparks before her—someone pushing her in a swing, soft hands picking her up, laughter and sunlight under the trees.

"I look at pictures sometimes," she said wistfully. "Mama was very pretty. I wish I looked more like her. Papa was tall and he always smelled like pipe tobacco and peppermints."

Bobby looked down at her, profiled against the fire. "Oh, Red," he said sadly. "We're more alike than I knew."

She twisted her head around and looked up at him. "Was she pretty?"

"Who?" he said blankly. "Oh, my mother. Yeah, she was pretty." He laughed a short, mirthless laugh. "Too pretty to be saddled with a kid, so most of the time I got palmed off on anyone who had a free afternoon. Or night. Or left alone in some dump of a hotel room."

"Oh, Bobby, that's awful. That's—I'm sorry, I didn't know it was like that."

He reached out and brushed the hair off her face, then blushed slightly and tucked his hands under his elbows, folding his arms across his chest. His mouth lifted in the old teasing smile, and he said, "Jeez, Red, it ain't the end of the world. I just wanted you to know there're worse things than being stuck in one place. It was a long time ago, anyway."

They were silent for a few minutes, listening to the rain and the corn, popping gently in the forgotten basket. Miranda picked up the long handle and poked it toward the fire. "When this is done," she said, "why don't we take it in to Mary and see if we can cheer her up 'til Jerry gets back?"

"Swell idea. Say, were you serious about the long green? Oughta be good for a coupla cans of film."

"Uh-huh," she said, her eyes on the basket. "I haven't wanted to run away for weeks now. Not since you all came."

"Then let's go cheer up the Boss, too," Bobby said brightly. "Nothing," he yawned, stretching his arms over his head, "cheers up good old C.J. like cold cash."

That night, as Lucy sat reading in the pool of light from the lamp on the alcove table, Miranda came up behind her. She put her arms around Lucy's neck and kissed the top of her head.

"What was that for, darling?" said Lucy, touched and a little surprised.

"Oh, nothing much, Auntie, I just wanted to tell you that, oh, that—"

"That sometimes your old Auntie's not so bad?" She took off her wire-rimmed spectacles and placed them on the table. She turned in her chair and wrapped her arms around Miranda's waist. "Sometimes you're not so bad yourself, darling girl."

They stayed for a time in quiet embrace, a tableau in the dim room, the only sound the wet leaves slapping the windows as the storm died. Maybe she's growing up, Lucy mused. She's been so agreeable the past few weeks, less willful somehow.

Miranda watched the lamplight turn the loose curls around Lucy's face into a golden haze, and thought of a sad-faced little boy with dark hair, alone in a dreary hotel room.

Cut to the Chase

The American Moving Picture Company stood in their lot and surveyed the damage. The air was crisp and sweet and fresh, as it always is after summer storms of such fury, but C.J.'s words were neither sweet nor fresh. They were, however, crisp.

"This is the end!" stormed the voice that had once reached the last row of the top balcony. "The ever-lovin', gold-plated, brass-tailed, putrescent, pluperfect living end!"

"Take heart, Boss," Jerry said. "It's not that bad."

"Not that bad?" A vein pulsed at his temple. "Perhaps some events in the History of the World have been worse, but I would . . . not . . . know. I was not at Waterloo, Gettysburg, or Little Big Horn. Nor was I on the *Titanic*." He lit a cigarette, snapping the match on his thumbnail, and jabbed it toward the stage. "Life was simpler in the circus. If the tent fell you moved on."

"You were in the circus too?" said Miranda.

"I had a trained animal act." He glowered at her. "Hence my skill with actors."

"Hey, Boss, listen," Bobby said. "Red and I took a look around before you came out, and we had an idea."

"Oh, joy," said C.J. "Advice from the nursery. Well, well, speak up. This is no time to go all shrinking violet on me."

"Okay," Bobby said affably. "Here goes. It doesn't matter about the dining room—"

"Have you gone made or just blind? There's a *tree* through the floor. Farmers live there, boy, not Wagnerian gods."

"We can do the rest of the dining room shots in the house," Bobby said. "And since we already shot the murder we don't need the barn anymore. See?"

"We should be glad the tree didn't wreck more than it did," Miranda added.

"Thank you, Pollyanna," C.J. said acidly, and turned to scowl at the stage. The drapes were heavy with damp, and had dragged the wires into dejected arcs, but the sun would soon dry them and the wires could be tightened. The cubicles, however, were a dead loss; boards had splintered, canvas had ripped, and the rain had washed painted reality to Impressionist daubs. "At least," he said after a minute, "we don't have to contend with Black Bess today. She'd have a field day with this."

"I thought I heard you on the telephone with Miss McGill just now," said Mary. "Laughing fit to beat the band. What was all that about?"

"It seems one of the pylons was knocked out in the storm yesterday, and the ferry hit the dock like the crack of doom—"

"That was nothin'!" exclaimed Jerry. "Just a wee bump."

"Well, it put the fear of God into The Widow," said C.J. "Spending the day with the smelling salts, so My Pet said." He flicked his cigarette away and sighed, "The unavoidable awaits." He climbed onto the stage and picked his way across the debris and into the back of the platform. "Generator looks fine," he called over his shoulder. "When Mutt 'n' Jeff get here they can pull down the walls

at the far end; we can use the open space for the gallows." He muttered something, and a chair leg soared out and landed in the wet grass. "We'll shoot it natural," he shouted. "Late afternoon, shadows galore. Title it something like 'The Sun Sets on The Boy's Life and The Girl's Hopes'—oh, it'll be atmospheric as all getout." He rounded the torn wall of the dining room, and arched an eyebrow at Bobby. "Out of the mouths of babes. If we follow your plan all we have to repaint is the jail cell. We got enough Cooper-Hewitts for the job, Donnelly?"

Jerry lowered a slab of beefsteak from his left eye and calculated under his breath, "One bank, that's eight sets o' six tubes each. Room's ten by twelve. Split the bank, hang half down either side." He called, "Plenty 'lumination fer one room, Boss. Can do."

"Well, thank goodness for that," said Mary. "We can have a proper dining room again instead of taking all our meals in the kitchen like potato farmers." Jerry's laugh turned into a whimper and he replaced the steak over his eye. Mary frowned worriedly and said, "I'm going to fix you up some compresses—ice water and vinegar. That bit of meat'll only go so far," and she headed down the lot at a determined trot.

Jerry smiled sheepishly at Bobby and Miranda. "Fusses, she does."

With a silent shake of the head Bobby forestalled Miranda's question. "Tell ya later," he mouthed, and glanced at Jerry: Jeez, he looked terrible. He always said "Fightin's fer folks don't have any smarts," but what else could explain his swollen face and skinned knuckles?

Jerry had returned early that morning as they were sitting down to a decidedly gloomy breakfast. He had appeared in the doorway, swaying wearily and attempting a smile, clutching his tattered jacket closed so Mary would not see the dried blood spattering his shirtfront.

Bert McGraw's hurriedly telephoned tip had sent him to a rendezvous on the Brooklyn docks. The Trust was indeed "pulling

their old tricks again," buying up all the American-manufactured raw stock; film smuggled in from Europe was the one hope of the independents. A shipment had come in, but, unbeknown to Bert, a trap had been laid. "Them Pinkerton toughs again," Bobby had heard him tell C.J. in a low aside.

"Hid the car in an alley and waited the night away," Jerry had told them, forking down an enormous breakfast while Mary sobbed on his shoulder. "Dry them pretty eyes now. Got somethin' for me sweetheart," and he had pulled the unpawned wedding ring from his watch pocket. The little ruby in its nest of seed pearls had twinkled in the morning light as Jerry slipped it on her finger and kissed the rough red hand, and Mary had cried all the harder. Jerry had a black eye of majestic proportions, Mary had her ring, the backseat of the car was piled high with enough film to finish the picture—and Robert Ian Gilmer had learned long ago that some questions were better left unasked.

Al and Tony were delighted at the prospect of demolishing part of the stage, and not because it was easier than building it had been. No, it was just one more piece of evidence adding to the burden of proof that Charles Tourneur was a lunatic. They could understand why he wanted the lumber saved (they'd been in pictures long enough to know that the eleventh commandment was "Thou shalt not throw anything away"), but why did he have Donnelly and those two kids trucking it out the back gate and over to the yard behind the Company house?

Jerry mopped his forehead with his bandana and assessed the pile of two-by-fours next to the Model T. "That'll do 'er."

"Do what?" mumbled Miranda, sucking at the splinter imbedded in her thumb. If it didn't work loose she would have to go into the house and have Mary take it out with a sewing needle, and she might miss something.

"I think I know," said Bobby, eyes shining. "This oughta be some fun. You think this sad old flivver can support the weight?"

"Good Dee-troit steel, lad? Any day of the week, and it ain't

that old, anyhow. This fellah's just had a hard life." Jerry patted the hood as one would pat the rump of a favorite horse; a piece of metal fell from the undercarriage with a grating tinkle. He got in the car, unhooked the windscreen and folded it flat against the hood, and crawled out over the dashboard. He sighted down the hood, squaring his hands in the frame-finding gesture, then crawled out again and said, "Well, don't be standin' there gawpin'. Let's put the top down."

With a great deal of effort where some rusty buckles were concerned, and a considerable amount of dust released, the cloth top was pulled back and accordioned into place on the back of the car.

"Are we going for a drive, Bobby?" Miranda said, flapping the dust out of her skirt.

"You could say that, Red." He grinned at her. "In a manner of speaking."

"Right-o," said Jerry. "Bring me that box of nails, Missy, and that hammer. Robbie, pick out four two-by-fours and saw 'em to, let me see—" He took a folding ruler from a back pocket and measured from the running boards to the top of the hood. "Three feet exact." He measured the hood from the folded-down windscreen to the ornament atop the radiator grille, and said, "And two more at four foot. We'll attach the frame here, like a box fitted over the hood. Lay boards over that, nail 'em down true, and there ye'll have it. As sweet as pie."

"Have what, for Pete's sake?" said Miranda; they were always setting off into uncharted territory, leaving her by the side of the road with her thumb in her mouth.

"A camera platform!" said Bobby and Jerry, and reached across the hood to shake hands.

"You're gonna put Baby on the *car*?"

"Now, lass," said Jerry, "d'ye think I'd be lettin' harm come to Baby? We'll spread open her tripod, flatten it out like, and tie her down as fast as cee-ment. I'll lean out and crank 'er. Robbie'll drive."

Bobby turned away to hide his excitement. How he loved to drive! Only Miranda knew about the magazine page folded at the bottom of his makeup kit. (If he could keep her secrets she could darn well keep his.) The paper was creased and worn, and repeated caressing had dulled its slick surface: pictured was a shiny, wire-spoke-wheeled, brass-fitted, fire-engine-red Stutz Bearcat. Someday he was going to have that car and drive it as fast as it would go, and if Red behaved herself he might take her for a spin.

Miranda folded her arms in an unconscious imitation of Aunt Lucy at her most disapproving. "And where will C.J. be?"

"Standing up in the back like he was Ben-Hur," said Bobby.

"And where will I be?"

"On the streetcar, of course," answered Jerry.

"Oh," she said. "Is this another one of C.J.'s cockamamie ideas, like having you hit Bobby, or throwing me in the river?"

"Jeez, Red," said Bobby. "You sound like The Widow. You're supposed to be coming to my rescue. We don't have a horse and The Little Sister's too young to drive, so we settled on the streetcar. C.J. figured you'd know the routes, and could pick us out a nice long stretch. What could go wrong?"

What could go wrong, thought Miranda. She stood at the corner of Garfield and Crescent and looked at the shabby frame houses climbing the grade to the railroad tracks. "This is perfect," she said aloud. "Auntie and I don't know anybody on this side of town, so I won't get caught. C.J.'ll be happy, 'cause the tracks run almost straight past the mill to the end of the line."

She heard the bell, and straightened the pinafore and shoved the wide straw hat firmly down on her head. The breeze was blowing her hair right at her face, and she picked it off the greasepaint impatiently. Bobby had made her up and she liked Dulcie's method better. How could he stand that heavy stuff? She felt like one of the little frosted cakes Lucy made her pass around at musicales.

Clang-clang! Clang-clang! With a grinding of gears and a squeal

as the brakes grabbed the steel rails in the pavement, the streetcar stopped at the corner. She glanced quickly to her left. They were right behind, as promised, pulled in close to the curb so Jerry could shoot her getting on board.

She looked straight ahead, the nickel cool in her damp palm. She grabbed the brass handrail and pulled up the wooden stairs, scooped into shallow *U*'s by years of ascending and descending feet. Smiling politely at the conductor, she dropped the coin in the box beside him. "Go to the rear platform," C.J. had instructed, "and when you get out there carry on like the fate of the world was in your hands. As you burst into tears at the drop of a hat that should pose no difficulty."

Miranda was halfway down the aisle, paying no attention to the passengers on the narrow seats under the windows, when a shrill voice called her name.

"Miranda Gaines. What are you doing here?"

She stopped, and grabbed the center pole to keep from stumbling. Think fast, she thought frantically. Act like you have a perfect right to be here. She attempted to wipe all but well-brought-up politeness from her face, then turned. "Good afternoon, Mrs. Duncan. How are you this afternoon? I hope you are fine."

Emma Duncan folded her hands together on the large cardboard box on her lap. "I asked you a question, Miranda. What are you doing here?" She took a closer look. "What in tarnation is that goop on your face?"

"Uh—I got poison ivy," said Miranda, struck with the kind of inspiration born of terror. "I was playing in the woods and I got a terrible case of poison ivy. It's cal-ci-mine lotion."

"If you say so," Emma snorted. "You look a perfect hussy, but I suppose even Lucy wouldn't let you paint. She does let you run wild, if you ask me."

Miranda bit back the urge to say "Nobody did ask you," and said, quite sweetly, "What's in the box, Mrs. Duncan?"

"I am taking one of my very special Lane cakes to a poor family

in Milltown," Emma said smugly. "We must take care of those less fortunate in this world."

Miranda grabbed the pole again as the streetcar rounded a corner. She knew Mrs. Duncan's Lane cakes. They were not light, and were larded with what Auntie called "those celluloid fruit cubes." "But if they don't have anything to eat, wouldn't it be better to take them bread, or some soup?" she asked.

"I wouldn't expect someone like you to understand the concept of Christian charity," Emma said. "When I think of what—"

"Excuse me, Mrs. Duncan, but I don't feel well. I'm going to go out back and get some air." C.J. must be furious; the footage they must be wasting while she was trapped in here with this old bat. Poor Jimmy—Bobby knew what he was talking about when he said some parents were worse than being an orphan. She turned and ran for the back of the car.

"You come back here this minute, you rude child."

Miranda opened the gate that let onto the back platform and looked down into the street. Jerry was cranking away at poor Baby, who lay roped to the camera platform like a heroine trussed to the train tracks. Bobby was hunched blissfully over the wheel, dreaming of the Indianapolis Speedway as he changed gears more than was strictly necessary. C.J. was precariously braced against the folded-down roof, screaming through his megaphone. "Where is that kid? I swear I'll—" He spotted her and shouted, "Wave your arms! Emote! Emote!"

Miranda leaned over the railing. Her hair was unbraided (more dramatic for this scene, they had decided), and it fanned over her shoulders in a flaming cloud. She clasped her hands to her breast in despair, then flung them wide. This was glorious! The air felt wonderful after the stuffiness inside, and she knew she was creating the desired effect, for the Boss was shouting, "Good, good!"

"What are you doing out here, waving your arms around like a wild Indian?"

Rats!

Emma grabbed Miranda's arm. "Come back inside this minute."

"I told you I'm going to be *sick*," she yelled at Emma, then turned and threw herself across the railing and mouthed "Help!" Emma looked down into the street and shrieked, "Land sakes, it's those trashy flickers people—they're following us!" She tugged Miranda's arm. "Get back inside, get back inside. They'll see us." C.J. was bellowing, "Great! Great! I love it!"

Miranda yelled, "Leave me alone, you!" and wrenched her arm out of Emma's grasp. Emma grabbed for her again. The string loop holding the cardboard box over her arm snapped and the box fell to the platform. "My cake," Emma cried, and dived for it. The streetcar rocked as they approached another bend in the route and Miranda fell over Emma. She banged into the back wall of the car and slid to the floor.

Think fast, think fast. "O-o-oww," she howled, "you hurt me." She gave Emma her best look of injured innocence. "What were you trying to do, Mrs. Duncan?" she said pathetically. "I was just taking a ride to amuse myself 'cause Auntie has lessons all afternoon. Those people weren't bothering me." She trembled her chin and massaged her shin through her torn stocking. "I think you broke my leg."

Emma straightened her hat and tucked the cake box under one arm. "Oh, stop whining," she snapped. "I did nothing of the kind." The streetcar slowed and the bell rang. "This is my stop." She stepped over Miranda's legs and crossed the platform, then turned back at the stairs, leaning down and shaking her finger for the parting shot. "You've always been a smart-alecky little baggage, Miranda. No child of *mine* would be allowed to go gallivanting around town, I can tell you. You go straight home now, and if that aunt of yours won't do anything about keeping you under control— well! we'll just see." And she marched down the stairs.

"Yes, ma'am." Miranda stuck her tongue out at the retreating back, then leaned against the swaying car and closed her eyes. I can

tell Aunt Lucy I was minding my own business and Emma butted in, she thought. She'll believe that. Auntie's always so ladylike, but I don't think she likes Old Lady Duncan any more'n I do.

They were waiting for her at the end of the line. The streetcar rotated in front of the car barn, then stopped. Miranda descended on the legs of a newborn foal and wobbled over to the dusty black Ford. C.J. vaulted over the side of the car and enfolded her in a bear hug. He lifted her up, whirled her around, and joyously proclaimed, "That was the funniest thing I've ever seen!"

He put her down and she stared at him. "It was funny? I thought you'd be mad at me for wrecking the shot." She turned to Jerry for confirmation.

"Cannot wait to see them dailies," he chuckled.

"The last time I saw anything that funny," Bobby said, "was in a Charlie Chaplin picture— Here we go," he said, grinning. "She's gonna ask who Chaplin is."

She sank onto the running board. "Can we go home now?"

They drove back to Pine Street via Miranda's suggested route, one well away from the streetcar line; what if Emma, returning from Milltown, happened to look out the window and see her in the car with "those trashy flickers people"?

C.J. and Jerry adjourned to the laboratory (the bedroom adjoining the projection room) for a quick develop on the afternoon's footage. The rest of the weary Company sat around the kitchen table, feasting on bread-and-butter and lemonade. "Isn't it amazing," Miranda said contentedly, "how washing your face and getting something to eat can make you feel like a whole new person?" and reached for her third sandwich. Bobby pushed up the tip of his nose with a forefinger and made oinking sounds in the back of his throat.

"Yoo-hoo," C.J. sang down the stairwell. "Curtain's going up!"

In companionable silence they sprawled on the chairs and watched The Little Sister board the streetcar and, after a lengthy

pause, rush onto the back platform and fling her arms to the wind.

"Look at all that hair," Mary murmured.

"Just like the figurehead on a ship," Jerry said.

"Speaking of ships," said C.J. from the back of the room, where he stood cranking the projector with one hand, a cigarette in the other, "enter *Old Ironsides.*"

And there was Emma Duncan, pinned to the wall by Jerry's cinematography like a stout butterfly. Bobby sniggered and pulled Miranda's hair, and she tittered nervously. Then Emma bent over to retrieve her Lane cake, and Miranda wrapped her arms around her waist and guffawed until her sides ached. Who would ever have suspected that Mrs. Duncan, the starchiest of the starchy, the primmest of the prim, wore striped drawers under those dowdy skirts? It was more of a revelation than The Widow's purple stockings. Too bad she couldn't share it with Auntie.

"Who *is* that frightful harpy?" C.J. asked of the air over his head.

"That," Miranda said grandly when she got enough breath, "is the local harridan and troublemaker" (she rolled the *r*'s), "one Emma Duncan, known to all and sundry as Old Lady Duncan."

C.J. choked on his cigarette; Bobby flashed his lopsided grin at her and looked as pleased as if he'd said it himself.

"Blessed Mother-of-us-all," Jerry said, "she's startin' to sound like the very Boss himself."

"Just like you," said Mary, "to take pleasure in turning a sweet little girl—"

"Her?" Bobby hooted.

"As I was saying, to take pleasure in turning a sweet little girl into a hammy old movie like yourselves." But she smiled.

"That was a real treat, Boss," Bobby said as he stood and turned on the overhead light. "Too bad we can't use it. Slapstick doesn't fit in with The Little Sister's mission much."

"Not so fast, Robert," C.J. said. "It occurs to me that after the murder we have The Boy's arrest and trial, Dulcinea weeping all

over creation—enough tragedy for two dime novels and an opera. A laugh injected into the tension at this point would give the audience some relief, make 'em sit up for the end."

"But what would that woman be doing there?" Bobby persisted. "Who is she supposed to be?"

"Couldn't she just be a snoopy old busybody?" Miranda said. "Someone who doesn't like me—The Little Sister—and wants to stop her from rescuing The Boy?"

"You've got something there, Missy," said C.J. "If all else fails try the truth, I always say; and you did say she was a troublemaker. What's the story on this woman, anyhow? Will she want billing? Or—God help the budget—money?"

"If I were you, Boss," she said, "I wouldn't even let her know she's in the picture. Mrs. Duncan—well, she goes around telling everybody how they should behave all the time, busting in when she's not invited. . . . " She glanced at Bobby, and said uncomfortably, "She's sort of been the ringleader lately. Against—against—"

"Against what, dear?" said Mary.

"Against you, all of you. I think she's the one who convinced my—convinced everyone to—to be against show people." She turned to Mary and said, "That's why she was so mean to you in the Emporium. I'm sorry."

"She's a perfect tartar, that one," Mary said. "But surely she didn't convince everyone. Your aunt let you join the Company, after all."

"Sure she did," Bobby jumped in, and Miranda glowed with gratitude. "And anyway, the woman's sick, remember? You know she doesn't care what Red does."

All during this exchange a satisfied smile had been spreading across C.J.'s face. "Emma Duncan, eh?" he said, and slapped his thigh. "The penny drops at last! All afternoon it's been like a sore tooth. Why was that rather noticeable silhouette so blasted familiar? The first week we were here—"

"Not her!" Bobby exclaimed. "No—really? The one who read you the riot act?"

"Threatened me with sixteen kinds of damnation if we didn't muzzle the noise. No wish to tangle with the natives, as I said, but there was no talking to her. Finally bid her good day and showed her the door. So she doesn't think much of theatricals, eh?" He fixed on Miranda. "Tell your Uncle C.J. what mean old Mrs. Duncan has been saying about us."

Miranda twisted her fingers together and looked down. "I don't want to hurt your feelings," she said.

"Oh, my very dear girl," he said warmly. "This is hardly news. We've all felt the slings and arrows of outrageous prejudice. Why, not so long ago actors weren't even allowed burial in hallowed ground—and the establishments barring us entry are legion. Jealousy, probably. Who wouldn't rather strut and fret the stage than slave at some dull-as-ditchwater job? If Emma's the dragon you say, then what finer revenge than to put her in a moving picture?"

"Oooh," she said. "I never thought of that."

"Indeed." He chuckled evilly and twirled an imaginary mustache. "Better than catching Carrie Nation drunk on the barroom floor, say I. That'll teach her to mess with The American Moving Picture Company!"

Hold for Close-up

Mary wanted a bonnet. Not a sunbonnet, mind, but an old-fashioned poke bonnet to hide her face from the camera. "I'm no actress, I can't do it—and you can stop with the calf eyes, Charles."

Double and triple duty was the order of the day. Jerry's windfall had helped, but the Company exchecquer had emptied steadily until, finally, they were left with the inventive scrambling to make a penny do the work of a dollar. And no, C.J. would not accept Miranda's twenty-eight dollars. He had not taken it the day of the storm, he would not take it now, he would not take it ever: "Rob a child's penny bank? Not even I will stoop that low."

If it took a bonnet to put Mary before Baby's all-seeing eye, then a bonnet she would have. There were, Miranda said, plenty of old hats in her attic. She made her usual circuitous way home, and was halfway down the front hall when Lucy called her into the parlor.

Lucy was in the wing chair beside the davenport, twisting and untwisting her handkerchief. She studied the girl, her face expressionless, then said, "Do you have something to tell me?"

Miranda felt the blood leave her face. She licked her lips. "A hat," she whispered. "I wanna borrow a—"

"Mrs. Duncan was just here. For an hour. Now would you like to tell me what happened Monday afternoon?" She settled back in the chair. "I'm waiting."

Miranda closed her eyes briefly and thought, Anger—that's how I'll play it. "Oh, she makes me so mad!" she said boldly, stamping her foot. "I was ridin' the streetcar 'cause I was bored and she insulted me and followed me all over. Then she sat on me."

Lucy made an odd snorting sound, then said firmly, "She said you were extremely rude. She also said you were waving to the flickers people off the back platform."

"I was not! You know Mrs. Duncan thinks people are being rude when they're only being truthful. And—and I didn't even know they were the flickers people 'til she started screaming at me. She scared me half to death, Auntie. . . ." Miranda forced herself to look her aunt in the face, and held her breath.

"I cannot go through any more with that woman," Lucy said wearily. "Do me a favor—stay as far away from her as you can."

"Will I!" Miranda said giddily. "I'll stay so far away from her she'll forget my name. Please, may I be excused? I have to get a hat from the attic. The gang's doing a play."

"As long as it's not *The Man in the Iron Mask* again," said Lucy. "Nothing with armor—remember what happened last time."

"I still say that wasn't my fault," said Miranda. "How was I s'posed to know that ol' bucket'd get stuck on Jimmy's head?"

"Do I need Mrs. Duncan over here twice in one day?"

"I won't do anything like that again, I promise," Miranda said, and turned for the safety of the hall, Lucy calling after her: "And stay off the streetcar!"

Once in the attic, she went straight to the "rainy-day junk trunk." Lucy had assembled the collection of molting feather fans, ripped shawls, and corset covers for dress-up sessions with the Fel-

lowes girls, periodically adding out-of-date items or unsuccessful sewing projects. There was nothing new today—and no hats. Miranda then pawed her way through Grandmother Gaines's steamer trunk—all that musty black silk made her think of The Widow—and the box with the sneeze-inducing uniforms Grandfather and Great-Grandfather had worn in the Civil and Mexican wars. She was about to leave when she spotted a small trunk wedged into a dark corner under the eaves. I don't think I ever looked in there, she thought.

She crawled into the corner, knelt before the trunk and flipped up the brass flap over the keyhole. The lid lifted with a protesting *screee-e-eee*, and a moth flitted out and batted a crazy path through the dust-laden air. A layer of tissue paper was tucked around the contents; she pulled aside the frail sheets, and gasped.

The bodice of the gown was pale pink satin, and, as silk will do with time, was going to threads; the whalebone stays around the narrow waist peeked through the fraying fabric. The sleeves were gossamer poufs of tulle trimmed with rosebuds of artfully folded satin ribbon—once crisp and airy and gay, now limp and freckled with rust.

She stood and raised the dress as far as she could reach. Tiny tarnished jewels sprinkled down the gown caught the low light as the skirt rose past the rim of the trunk, tier upon cascading tier of ruffles. A swath of rose satin draped the hips, swept into a saucy bustle at the back, and ended in a large crushed bow. The lace edging the neckline was stained with something oily, and caked with powder: Miranda brought it to her face, and sniffed.

"Makeup," she whispered, "but not like Dulcie's." This smelt of the old-fashioned theatrical makeup Bobby used, the fat fruity-smelling sticks in the brown paper tubes. There was a trace of another aroma under the greasepaint and powder—the mildewy sweetness of lavender.

She laid the dress back into its bed of tissue, struck with the

feeling that she was disturbing something best left undisturbed. It was lovely and ruined and rather sad, like a packet of brittle love letters tied with faded ribbon.

As she reached up to close the trunk a paper tucked under the lid fluttered onto the gown. She picked it up and held it to the beam of sunlight slicing the dim attic. It was a small handbill, brown with age and split along the folds. Haltingly, she read aloud:

——*The Majestic Theatre*——
49 Cleveland Boulevard, Topeka, Kansas
. . . .

The Management Is Proud to Present:
Mademoiselle Lucille & Monsieur James
Expert Exponents of Terpsichore
Olde-style Ballads & Genteel Patter
July 23–27, 1894
—Six shows daily—
. . . .

Dine at The Harrison Hotel after the show!
——Two doors to the left of The Majestic——
Midnight Suppers a Speciality of the House
. . . .

It must be Lucille's dress, she thought. Who was she? Auntie's name's Lucinda, and she was never in Kansas, anyway, or in the theater. And Mama's name was Martha Anne. . . . She slid the paper back under the strap, closed the trunk, and descended the ladder into the upstairs hall. "I'm sorry, Mary," she said later, "I guess we didn't have a bonnet after all."

C.J. put an arm around Mary's shoulders. "Now that I think of it, we'll just shoot you with your back to Baby. A shawl over your head, a basket on your arm—why, it'll read Sweet Old Mother as plainly as a sign around your neck."

"Scoot back, lad," Jerry called to Bobby, who was sitting on a

bench in the repainted jail set. "Just a—stop. See, Boss?" he said, pointing to the light slanting down from the barred window high in the back wall. "Hits his head; makes a halo."

"If that doesn't say 'innocence unjustly imprisoned' . . . half my work's done," C.J. said delightedly. "Roll camera, you clever devil. A-a-and action!"

He lowered his voice. "Look despondent, boy. They're going to hang you at sundown. Think back over your whole miserable life and remember every rotten thing that ever happened . . . every wrong done you . . . every rejection . . . every lonely hour."

"Oh, that's not fair," Miranda whispered to Dulcie. "That's so mean." They sat together at the side of the set, out of camera range. "Shhhh," Dulcie whispered. "Charlie knows what he's doing. Bobby's a professional."

And, right before their eyes and Baby's lens, Bobby's face changed, gradually, into the bleak landscape of remembered pain Miranda had seen the afternoon by the fire. So that was why C.J. said that, she thought. It was cruel, but it had worked.

"Mistress Mary," C.J. directed, "enter now. *Slowly.* Robert, keep your head low. Mary, I want you to stand there and let all that maternal compassion of yours well up in your tender breast. Now kneel before him. Good. Robert, raise your head—slowly, slowly, as if you cannot bear the weight—and look into her eyes."

Bobby lifted his head and placed a hand on Mary's cheek. She covered his hand with hers and leaned into it and whispered something. He raised his face into the beam of light, then looked back into her face, and Miranda saw tears on his painted cheeks.

The scene moved with the drugged, deliberate tempo of suspended time. Jerry leaned on Baby as he cranked, a trancelike expression on his face. C.J.'s directions were velvety and slightly remote, as though they came from somewhere a long way off: "Oh, my boy, my boy. Yes. Yes. Your heart is breaking. You will never see her again . . . your dear mother, who loves you better than anyone in the world. . . ."

"Oh, stop," Miranda breathed. "Oh, stop, please stop." Dulcie was weeping quietly, a hand pressed to her mouth.

Bobby took Mary's face in his hands and leaned over and kissed her forehead, then lifted his face again to the beam of light as if the very salvation of his soul lay in its dusty brightness. Mary sank to the floor and laid her head on his lap. Her face was toward C.J. and Jerry, her terror of the camera forgotten. Slowly, as slowly as a feather falls to earth, Bobby came down from the light and laid his head on her shoulder. His thin hands wound convulsively in the folds of her shawl. The breeze rustled through the trees over the set and a car went down the street; it turned the corner onto Broad and the sound died away. Across the street Nell Fellowes called "Carrie, Carrie-e-e" in her childish treble. Bobby's wracking sobs subsided into silence. C.J. waited, then whispered "Cut." Jerry kept cranking. C.J. cleared his throat and repeated "Cut"—and the spell was broken.

Bobby lifted his wet face and looked around as if he had no idea where he was. He blinked and looked down at Mary huddled on his lap, then at C.J.

C.J. wiped his face with his scarf and said, "My God, boy. Why didn't you tell me you were going to do that?" His voice was hoarse.

"It was okay?" Bobby said shyly.

"My God." He lit a cigarette with shaking hands, then said in more normal tones, "That, dear boy, should rip the stone-cold heart out of every mother's son in the house. I knew you were good, but I didn't know you were *that* good."

Miranda watched from the sidelines as they flipped embarrassed jokes at one another, shaking off the scene the way a dog shakes off water. Bobby bantered with Mary as he helped her to her feet, but his laughter sounded forced and, makeup notwithstanding, he was still quite pale. It was wonderfully sad, Miranda thought, but I'm not so sure it was acting.

The last big scene of the picture was scheduled for the afternoon: "The Boy Goes to His Death." Jerry would play The Hang-

man. Imposing size was the major requirement for the role, and with his head covered by a black hood no one would know The Father had risen from the grave to oversee the execution of his murderer. C.J. would forgo breeches and boots for suit and string tie to portray The Hanging Judge. Al had won the toss, and would wear the policeman's uniform; Tony and the rest of the Company would be crowd "extras," all shot from behind. "Infinitely more effective that way," C.J. said, to which Bobby added, "And from the front you could tell it's just us."

C.J. went to the top of the steps and clapped his hands smartly. "Children, children! I shall be up here for this scene—trouping the boards again, as it were—so pay attention. The Boy will come up the stairs here, attended by The Law. Robert, take off your jacket— oh, Lor'."

"What's the matter?" Bobby said, twisting his head around to look down his back. "Have I got dirt on me?"

"What you don't have is muscles," C.J. said despairingly. "The biggest moment in the picture, and what'll the audience be doing? Trying to figure out if you eat more than once a month."

"Undershirts," said Mary. "That'll help."

There was a pause while all the men took off their jackets and shirts, stripped off their undershirts, and handed them to the chagrined boy. He repaired behind a large tree, emerging several minutes later. "Hmm," said C.J. "A tad lumpy, but it'll do." He put the megaphone to his mouth. "As I was saying, Robert will come up onto the platform. He will look out over the crowd, then Al will lead him to The Hangman. Just as Jerry places the noose around his neck, you, Miss Miranda, will come barreling up the steps, hot off the trolley, to tell The Judge that it has all been a tragic mistake. Everybody set? Good. Let's do this in one—we dare not send Donnelly back to darkest Brooklyn."

Miranda stood at the edge of the imagined crowd and watched The Boy walk up the steps to the gallows, his hands tied behind him. He was a black ink drawing on white paper: white shirt, black

pants, white skin, black hair. His hair was loose and ungreased, as it had been for the scene in the jail cell, and the crisp curls tumbled over his high forehead. Miranda thought he looked like the hero of every book she had ever read.

When her cue came, The Little Sister raced up the steps two at a time and flung herself at The Judge, shouting "Stop, stop!" She pointed to The Boy. "He's innocent!" She pointed to her chest. "I saw it, it was an accident!" She pointed to The Hangman. "Let him go free!" She pointed to The Judge, who struck his temples with great force. The Judge gestured to The Hangman, who removed the noose from The Boy's neck and untied his hands. The Little Sister threw herself on The Boy, who stood tall and looked with manly understanding over her head at The Judge. The Judge strode over to The Boy, shook his hand, and yelled, "Cut!"

C.J. went to the edge of the platform and called down to Dulcie. "Your turn, My Pet. Run up the stairs and over to Robert, then we'll reset for the close-up."

After The Girl had raced up the stairs with flowered skirts flying, Baby, Bobby, and Dulcie were repositioned. "Now," C.J. announced, "when she reaches The Boy all the other people vanish."

"Where do they go?" asked Miranda. She was sitting on the edge of the stage, sharing a cheese sandwich with The Mother.

"It's symbolic," he said, in the tone of voice one would use to explain long division to a very young or very dim child. "When The Boy and The Girl are together at last, it is as if they were the only two in the world." He turned to the young lovers. "When we roll I want you to take this bewitching damsel in your arms and kiss the bejesus out of her. Got it? Good. Action!"

Dulcie smiled sweetly at Bobby and placed her hands on his padded chest. Her cheeks dimpled and her eyes sparkled. She tossed her head and the hat fell down her back, caught by the velvet streamers. "Lovely touch," C.J. chuckled. "De-li-ci-ous."

Then Bobby put his arms around Dulcie—and no amount of

theatrical intuition could compensate for being fifteen. This bore little resemblance to the thwarted spooning on the front porch. He had her at last, but what was he supposed to do with her? He ducked his head and pecked Dulcie's mouth. He came up scarlet, swallowed twice, and looked uncertainly at C.J.

"Cut!" C.J. rubbed a hand over his head; smooth pate or no, he looked exactly like a man tearing his hair out.

"What," he said, "do you think you were doing?"

"Kissing her?"

"Oh, good God," he snapped. "That's not how you kiss a beautiful woman. Give 'er here!"

He crossed from Baby to Bobby in two steps. He moved the boy to one side and stood before Dulcie. "Watch closely," he said, and smiled down at her. She returned his smile and nodded encouragingly. Miranda leaned forward; this promised to be, as Bobby would have said, "some fun."

"You can't just dive for the girl as if she were dinner," he said. "First you look at her. See how the sun glints off her hair? That golden hair. Men have killed over hair like that. And those eyes! You could drown in that blue.

"Take her in your arms," he continued, "but slowly. The whole point is to savor every luscious moment, not tear through it as if you had a train to catch." Dulcie put her hands on C.J.'s broad chest and gazed into his eyes. He looked into her eyes, put his arms around her, and said in a distracted voice, "Then you kiss her." And he did. Dulcie stood on tiptoes; her tiny hands crept across C.J.'s shoulders to the back of his neck and stayed there. He bent her over his arm until her feet were on solid ground, then a little further. Her knees buckled.

"Look behind you," Mary hissed into Miranda's ear, and together they turned and looked down from the platform. The Widow was up and out of her chair. Her hands were clenched at her hips, her face was a dull red, and her breath whistled through gritted

teeth. Miranda signaled to Bobby, and pointed wildly. He looked at Mrs. McGill, then Miranda, and dread passed between them: the cat was forever out of the bag, and no cat ever had sharper claws.

Jerry noticed all the frenzied semaphore and turned to see Bessie stalking toward the platform with murder—certainly mayhem—in her slitted eyes. "Cut!" he yelled. "Fer the love o' God, Boss, *cut!"*

Dulcie and C.J. did not move. The Widow advanced. "Cut!" Bobby yelled, then Miranda, then Mary, until the entire Company was shouting. Finally they separated. Dulcie's face was flushed and she seemed to have forgotten how to breathe. There was a round of applause mixed with catcalls and whistles, and Jerry edged around to block the stairs. Mary darted under his arm, down the steps, and over to Bessie. Whatever she said reduced the heat from boil to simmer, for she was allowed to escort The Widow back to her chair.

C.J. tore his gaze off Dulcie and looked at Bobby. "Now that," he panted, "is how you kiss a pretty girl. We go again."

Bobby was talked through The Kiss, and he did manage to slow down and appear relaxed. After several takes he warmed to the task, and C.J. raised a pleased eyebrow to Miranda. "See, Missy? It's as I told you the first day: sometimes you have to let enthusiasm take the place of experience. Cut, you two."

He walked to the center of the stage and raised his hands. He waited until the Company quieted, then said grandly, "Thank you all very much, gentle ladies and kind gentlemen. That, my fine friends, was the last shot!"

Bobby leapt into the air with a yell. Jerry tossed his cap skyward and kissed Baby.

What a fuss, thought Miranda, just over the last shot of the day. "What're we gonna shoot tomorrow, Boss?" she asked.

"Not the last shot today, Red," Bobby said and grinned at her. "The last shot of the picture!"

Something lurched under her ribs; she buried her face in the blue pinafore, then looked up at Bobby. "It's all over?" she wailed. "We're d-d-*done*?"

"Oh, Jeez," he snickered. "Hey, Boss— Red thinks we're done 'cause we finished shooting."

"Oh, lass, if only that were true," said Jerry.

"Listen up, child," C.J. said grimly. "We have to edit the picture, cut it. For your information, that means," and he ticked off each item on his fingers, "slam the rough cut together, write and shoot the titles, assemble the master, produce the prints with each scene individually tinted, time the projection instructions and musical score cues, and *then*—God and those cretins at The Film Exchange willing—sell the bloody thing. And, lest we forget, come up with a brilliantly appropriate name for it. We're not done by a long chalk. Another two weeks at least."

"Two weeks," she sighed.

"Two weeks," said Jerry, and hastily crossed himself; he knew what was coming. "If we live that long."

Five Reels and a Prayer

C.J. had changed. Gone was the avuncular fellow who orated with the fire of a snake-oil salesman, and joked like the favorite uncle who bought you ice cream before supper. In his place was a driven, hollow-eyed specter who rapped out commands as impatiently as he flicked tobacco shreds from his lower lip, the smoldering cigarette butt as much a part of the new C.J. as the rakish scarf had been a part of the old. It was simple, really. Shooting a picture was Heaven—cutting a picture was Hell.

The rough cut was upon them. Every scrap of the footage was viewed and reviewed, each frame fretted and fussed and fumed over—it only had to be the best picture ever made. The air was thick with smoke and curses; the diet was coffee and angst. "I'm hip-deep in grounds," said Mary. "We're up to six pots a day."

Gone were Al, Tony, and Georgie, their services no longer required or affordable. Their final task had been to strip the platform of all save poles and wires. The generator, the rolled-up muslin drapes, and the canvas flats had all been stored in the basement. "So they won't get weatherbeaten," was the explanation. "We'll drag it all back out for the next one." It made sense, but Miranda was saddened by the barren, purposeless stage.

Dulcie was gone as well, off to Fort Lee for extra work on a costume drama. She had telephoned one evening to tell them that her French court wig weighed twelve pounds and she was learning the gavotte. But she would be back. "And not a moment too soon," they all agreed, for her sunny disposition was missed.

Now Miranda's days were spent carrying trays upstairs and listening to Bobby complain. The titles couldn't be written until the rough cut was done, and the inactivity rankled. He offered his help; he even suggested a solution for a particularly thorny editing problem one morning.

"Get . . . out!" C.J. howled at him. "You're giving me the pip, standing over me like that. You think I don't know how to cut film? Out! Go play on the train tracks. Leave, scram, vamoose, hie thee hence. Donnelly!" he roared, and slammed the door to the lab in Bobby's face.

"Get him outta here, Missy," Jerry said, taking her aside. "Fer the sake of us all, an' me especial. He's a dear lad, but he's gonna drive us 'round the bend." And so Miranda led the bitterly protesting boy away, out into the summer day. He shoved his hands into his pockets, frowned at the overgrown backyard, and said, "So whadda ya do in this burg for fun, huh?"

"We-e-ll," she said, "we could go downtown and get an ice-cream soda—"

"Oh, swell," he snorted. "I can just see that. 'Who's your friend, Miranda?' 'Oh, just one of those sinful show people I'm supposed to stay away from.' Got any other ideas?"

"We could go down to the fort," she said. "See what the gang's doing today."

"Aw, what the heck," he said. "C.J.'s no fun, I'm not allowed to take the car by myself, and I read all my books ten times over."

"I tell you what," said Miranda. "You come with me now, and I'll lend you a ton of books, okay?"

It was not an immediate success. Spending time with Red was one thing; sitting on wet ground to play Old Maid with a bunch of kids was another. After suffering through two hands, Bobby tossed his cards onto the crate and said, "What're we playin' this for, anyway?"

"Whaddya mean by that?" Tommy said darkly.

"It's silly," said Bobby.

"Oh, Bobby, please," said Miranda. "It's just a game."

"Yeah, well, it's a baby's game," he replied. "Gimme the rest of the cards, Stowing, and one of those atrocious cheroots of yours. Time you guys learned how to play poker."

Jimmy stared at him. "We ain't allowed to play poker!"

"So who's to know?" Bobby grinned.

Late that afternoon Miranda sneaked Bobby into her house to choose the books, tiptoeing through the kitchen and down the hall to the front stairs. (It was a calculated risk; the back stairs squeaked.) Behind closed parlor doors Lucy was demonstrating the correct way to play a Brahms waltz. Miranda watched Bobby drink it all in: the polished floors bright with rag rugs, the cabbage rose–papered walls lined with framed engravings, and, glimpsed through the plush-curtained archway, the long dining room table and the breakfront laden with Grandmother Gaines's service for twelve. The cabinet on the landing stopped him, and he bent down to peer in at the ivory curios, Dresden figurines, and souvenirs from her parents' honeymoon tour of the Continent.

He followed her up the stairs and stood in the doorway to her bedroom with his hands behind his back.

"Hurry up," she whispered. "Pick out what you want."

"A windowseat, a four-poster bed, and an aunt who plays the piano like that?" he whispered. "Tough life, Red."

"Take lots of books, Bobby, please. Here," and she pulled him over to the bookcase. It was not his words that made her feel suddenly ashamed; it was the yearning on his face.

They were exiled for a week. Miranda made up for a summer

lost to filmmaking; returning, somewhat, to old interests and friends, even spending a drizzly afternoon making paper dolls with the neglected Carrie while Bobby finished *The Count of Monte Cristo* and started *Around the World in Eighty Days*.

Bobby made up, as best he could, for a childhood lost to dressing rooms and midnight trains: Miranda and Tommy taught him to swim, screaming and splashing and soaking in the cool willow-hung river until their fingers and toes wrinkled, lying spent on the bank afterward to watch the clouds scudding above the trees; he was initiated into The Pine Street Irregulars with full and solemn ceremony, and won honors in the daring raid on Pearl Stowing's plum trees; he gave endless poker lessons at the fort until Tommy and Jimmy were pronounced "good as any stagehand," and Miranda was sent for the jar of kitchen matches so they could play for stakes.

It was an idyllic interlude, and it ended one morning as rudely as it had begun. They were heading out the back door, pockets full of sandwiches, heads full of plans to dam the Matawan with two fallen trees and the roof off the fort.

"Where do you think you're going?" C.J. barked over his third cup of coffee. "If Donnelly's setting up to shoot titles, don't you think we should write the blasted things?"

"Can I stay too, Boss?" Miranda asked.

"If you can manage to keep your dainty mouth shut."

"Maybe I better go help Jerry instead," she said uneasily.

Jerry was in the laboratory, methodically laying out supplies on the worktable: squat bottles of gummy black printer's ink, a shallow wooden tray of metal letters to be chosen, locked in place, and inked for the printing plate, and a stack of thick white cards. Miranda knew the machine at the end of the table was a hand-operated printing press; there was one like it in the school office.

"That's for printing the titles, isn't it?" she asked. "How do they work, exactly?"

"They're just bits o' dialogue, comments on the action and such," he said. "Gets y' from one scene to the next. I print 'em up

on them boards, shoot each one with m' still camera, then reverse 'em so's they're white on black. Easier on the eyes that way. Then they go in front o' Baby—in that rack so they stay steady—fer as long as the Boss wants 'em onscreen. Only as long as it takes fer any nitwit to read 'em, says he. Likes films titled sparselike.''

"Has he named the picture yet?"

"As of this mornin' it's *The Romance of Red Fern Valley*," he said. "What d'ye think?"

She made her expression of socially acceptable politeness and answered, "Very nice, I'm sure."

"And what is that look on yer face?" he said, and Miranda blushed. "You little darlin', you really do have a naked face. Don't be actin' shocked now, it's just an old sayin'." He lifted her up onto the table, then bent down so his face was level with hers. "Have y'ever gotten away with a lie, Missy?"

Miranda was about to say "I don't lie" when her train of thought was derailed with one large red flag. What have I done all summer *but* lie, she thought. If I died tomorrow I'd probably go straight to Hell. Without stopping.

"That's it," Jerry chuckled. " 'Bout six expressions just flew by, like the sun dodgin' clouds. That's a naked face."

"Is that good?" she said seriously.

"Far as I can see," he said, thoughtfully stroking his mustache, "it's of no use to real life—get y' in trouble more times than not—but if yer after the movin' picture game there's no finer gift."

C.J. opened the door and said, "Well, do you want to see the rough cut or not?"

"Oh, yes, please," she said, and hopped down from the table.

It was not the thrill she had anticipated. She had been warned not to expect a finished picture, but this looked like nothing more than the best dailies, trimmed and strung in order.

Bobby scribbled rapidly, eyes darting between the wall and the pad on his lap. C.J. kept stopping the projector to wind scenes back so they could be re-viewed, spitting and snarling and smoking

around the pencil clenched between his teeth like a pirate's cutlass. He did want as few titles as possible, but he liked them verbose. Bobby didn't care how many there were as long as they were easily understood. "Who's the director?" C.J. yelled, and Bobby yelled back, "Who's the writer?" "Romance, boy, I want more romance!" "That gush sounds like something out of *Woman's Home Companion!*"

Technical phrases batted about the room like caged canaries. She knew what a close-up was, and a dissolve, but what was cross-cutting? Maybe they meant the jumping back and forth between the streetcar and the crowd around the gallows. Now was not the time to ask, and all the stopping and starting and arguing was making her head ache. It was a relief when The Kiss filled the wall, faded to black, and lunch was called.

The titles were completed by afternoon's end. Compromise won, C.J.'s vocabulary adding color, Bobby's simplicity adding strength. The Little Sister's entrance was heralded with:

> *And—as The Boy gazed upon his Dear One—*
> *the Skies opened o'er them . . .*
> *but sent forth neither rain nor hail nor sleet. . . .*

To Miranda's intense delight, the arrival of Emma Duncan on the back of the streetcar was titled:

> *As every town has old men to sit on the*
> *courthouse steps—and young girls to stroll*
> *by—so does every town have A Busybody.*
> *Large of girth, mean of spirit, and bent on Trouble. . . .*

While Jerry finished up, they trooped down to the kitchen for a cool drink. C.J. chose beer, and was in the middle of a rambling discourse on brewing techniques when the telephone rang. The weary authors moved not so much as an elbow from the table. Miranda's duties (sharpening pencils and delivering copy from one

room to the next) had been light, so she jumped up to answer. A familiar voice crackled down the wire.

She put her hand over the receiver and batted her eyes at C.J. "It's for you, Boss," she said coyly.

"My sweet Dulcinea!" C.J. brightened. "Stop acting like a demented Floradora Girl and give it here, wench."

Miranda handed him the telephone, then tiptoed over to Bobby and whispered into his ear.

"Hello-o-o-o?" C.J. cooed. "Oh, it's you." He put the receiver against his chest and hissed, "You die at dawn!" setting off a fizz of giggles.

"Yes, Madame, I know." The crackles rose perceptibly. "When the picture is sold, that's when you'll get your money."

"Dulcie's money, he means," Bobby said to Miranda.

"Why does she let Bessie push her around so much?" she asked.

" 'Cause she's her mother, I guess, or maybe she's scared to give her the brush."

"Excuse me, Madame." C.J. covered the receiver and said, "I assume you two want to eavesdrop, so pipe down." He returned to the call. "Pardon the interruption, I was uncorking another bottle of champagne. . . . No, I don't know when. It should go to The Exchange by the end of the week. . . . Spot bookings at first, but I have every confidence in a distribution deal." A look of suspicion came over his face. "What do you care so long as you get paid?" There was a long pause. "You *what*?"

"What, what?" said his audience.

"You drag her out to Griffith and I'll tell you exact—yes, out." Unexpectedly, he laughed. "Stay abreast of the times. The man's been in Los Angeles for a year, and I happen to know he's not casting. . . . Jerry got a letter from Billy, that's how. They're all tied up on some bloody great Civil War thing." He looked at the ceiling and said acidly, "Bitzer, dear. Billy Bitzer, the only cameraman better than Donnelly." He listened for a minute, then said vehe-

mently, "Agreed. Absolutely she'll get work, but she'll have to stand in line behind the Gish girls and Blanche Sweet and Mae Marsh for every blessed part and you know it. I can offer her more than third billing."

The crackles continued. With a sly smile he placed the business end of the earpiece on the receiver's brass maw. A high-pitched electronic whine pierced the air. Miranda and Bobby covered their ears and sniggered hysterically. C.J. put a finger to his lips and lifted the earpiece; the squawking could be heard all the way across the kitchen.

"So sorry," he said blandly. "There seems to be a problem with this line." The eyebrows met over a frown. "Let me remind you of one minor fact. We have a contract. You try to break it and I will bring a slime of shysters down on you like the wolf on the fold. Right. . . . We still have publicity stills to shoot. No. . . . Good-bye!" He banged the earpiece into the hook and set the telephone back on the hutch. "I think I know what did in the late Mr. McGill."

"She still trying to pry Dulcie loose?" Bobby said.

"In a nutshell," he said, and sat down at the table. "She's tone-deaf when it comes to the picture game. Superb credentials for a stage mother, eh? The *Sturm und Drang* I went through to get Dulcie here—no upstart independent would do. No, we should all be back at the Biograph, cranking out two-reelers and playing it safe. Artistic freedom be damned!" Their glasses jittered as he pounded the table. "That cuts no ice with The Widow. Why do you think D.W. went haring off to California—to pick oranges? To make the kind of pictures he wanted to, big pictures, features. Oh, they tried to keep him; built him a new studio, up on 174th Street in the Bronx. A thing of beauty, too. Remember?"

"Sure do," Bobby said. "Two big stages, one with natural light, one with artificial, dressing rooms, labs, all brand-new."

"Be a good boy, they said, play with your new toy. Good-bye Biograph, said he; cared more for freedom than floor space." The

storm subsided and he sat back and laced his fingers behind his head. "So do I, for that matter. So do we all, except The Widow; she cares only for the almighty dollar. There's not much she can do short of murder, however. Pity. The thought of Our Bessie in prison gray cheers me no end. . . ."

The ensuing days moved with the speed of a streetcar going off the rails, or a fall from a tree onto the pitched roof of a garden shed. When the titles were finished, Jerry spliced them into the negative of the rough cut to make the master, the all-important source of the prints to be released to theaters. The master was then separated into one-thousand-foot lengths for each of the five reels, and lovingly wound into steel cans marked DO NOT TOUCH—THIS MEANS YOU!

There was no time to bask in the warmth of accomplishment, no time to run the completed picture for Mary and Miranda. Finished release prints meant C.J. could begin the crucial selling phase. The sale of the initial prints would fund the manufacture of the incoming orders, and so on, and so on, until there was enough ready cash to start a new picture. That was the plan—that was what they lived for.

Making a print was complicated, finicky, and tiresome. First a section of negative and a corresponding length of unexposed film were fed, together, past the printing light in the darkened projection room. The exposed film then went to the lab for a series of baths, wound around a frame and lowered into a deep tin vat: developing and fixing solutions, clear water to remove all traces of the solutions, and a final treatment of glycerine and water. Each section was then dried on a large revolving drum, made of open slats so the air would circulate evenly.

Threading the film onto the drum and turning it was Miranda's job; if C.J. could shove seamstresses and stagehands in front of the camera, then Jerry could make lab assistants of fledgling actors. He tried to teach them to splice, but only Bobby's hands proved clever enough for the delicate task of scraping off the emulsion, lining up

the join by the sprocket holes, and applying the right amount of quick-drying cement to the cut ends. If not done perfectly the film would jump about on the screen, or, worst of all, break during projection.

When the film was dry it was cut apart again for the tinting process. Back it went into the tank, emptied of developer for a succession of murky soups with intriguing names: sulfide, ferrocyanide, vanadium. The gold-tinted scenes bathed together, then the blue, then the red; after, they were redried, respliced into finished prints, and tucked into their round steel beds.

"I thought it looked nice the way it was," Miranda ventured.

"You oughta see what it adds," Bobby told her. "When this dies down we'll run a print. Like the fight scene? Jerry did it red so it's all angry-looking, and you can make night shots just by tinting 'em blue. It's magic what it does."

Miranda's post as Musical Director was reactivated for the morning it took to devise a score, for what was a moving picture without music? They huddled over the Victrola, and the armload of sheet music she had "borrowed" off the top of the piano. C.J. hummed loudly (and flatly) as he timed it with a stopwatch. Eighteen bars here, eighteen bars there: sad songs for the sad scenes (Mary's suggestion of "Just Before the Battle, Mother" for the weeper in the jail cell met with "Genius!" from C.J. and a sigh from The Boy, so in it went), ragtime bounce for the comedy scenes, and the corny ballad from the first day of shooting to lead off the overture. No more than an outline was required. Any conductor worth his tailcoat would fill in the gaps, C.J. said, and in the smaller theaters the solo pianists beneath the screen would play whatever they chose.

The picture was named, finally, in an animated session. *The Romance of Red Fern Valley* had been deemed "a bore." *Murder on the Farm*? Nicely blunt, but where was the romance, or the humor? *The Love of a Boy and Girl*? Too obvious. *Love Saves the Day* came the closest, until Miranda huffily reminded them that

The Little Sister had saved the day—Love had caused all the trouble. How about *Love and the Little Sister*? "No, no," C.J. said hastily, "that'll give 'em the wrong idea entirely." Bobby stared into space, whispered *"Cupid and the Little Sister"*—and that was it.

Now Jerry could reshoot the main title (for the fifth time), splice it in, and C.J. would be ready to go. The cast credits were done, although eyebrows had been raised over Miranda's dogged insistence on a stage name. "Oh, let Red call herself that if she wants to," Bobby had championed. "If it's good enough for Alexandre Dumas . . . kinda pretty too, even if it does take two lines." So, in the end, the credit read: The Little Sister . . . Valentine de Villefort.

The next morning, while Jerry was being taught Old Maid at the kitchen table, C.J. called from the hall in the plummy tones of old. "Close your rheumy little eyes, my chickens." He entered the room. "Do let me dazzle you with the total effect. Open your eyes now. Slo-o-owly—start with the shoes and pan up."

"Spats?" said Miranda. "Golly!"

"Golly," echoed Bobby. "Get a load a Diamond Jim."

"Never, repeat never, throw away wardrobe," said C.J., and put his thumbs under his lapels and struck a pose. "Imbued with such sartorial splendor, do I or do I not look like someone you would buy a picture from?" He turned, grandly, to display the creamy linen suit, the snowy glare of the well-starched shirt, and the four-in-hand tie smoothed into the lapeled vest.

"Boss," Jerry said solemnly, "dressed like that you could be sellin' the Brooklyn Bridge."

"Don't give him any ideas, Jer'," laughed Bobby.

"Wait!" Miranda said. "Don't leave—wait!" She dashed out the back door and across the yard to the hedge, then dropped into a running crouch and sped to the rosebush under the parlor window. She picked one of Lucy's prized coral tea roses—the rubbery stem wouldn't break, so she pulled the branch down and used her teeth— and ran back, slammed open the screen door, slid across the kitchen to C.J., and panted, "For your buttonhole."

"Perfect!" he cried. "Perfection is details and details perfection, I always say." He pinched her cheek. "Now I can go. Fourteenth Street awaits. To those of you of the praying kind, I suggest you drop to your knees and spend the day ensuring our success." He snapped the brim of his hat to a debonair angle, tucked the five cans of *Cupid and the Little Sister* under one arm, and, with a full-speed-ahead-and-damn-the-torpedoes expression, marched out the back door.

Miranda had been taught to say her prayers every night, kneeling by her bed with folded hands and closed eyes. Her devotion was, for the most part, feigned. After she had finished off the Lord's Prayer she never knew what to say. You couldn't bring the dead back from Heaven, that much she knew, and you weren't allowed to ask for things like curly hair or new skates. Now she had something to ask for, although it was not quite what C.J. had intended.

"Please, God," she whispered. "Please let them stay next door forever and ever. Amen."

New York City

The morning of Miranda's birthday dawned hot and clear. She nestled lazily in the covers, then rolled over and patted around under the dust ruffle until she found it. She listened to make sure Aunt Lucy wasn't up and about, then drew it out and propped it on her knees. "It's the best present I ever got," she murmured.

"How did you know tomorrow's my birthday?" she had asked, and Bobby had winked. I'll bet Tommy told him, she had thought, staring at the package in her lap.

To a chorus of "Open it, open it!" she had pulled off the ribbon and torn away the tissue. A trembling "O-o-ooh" was all she had managed, for the old prickle had started. "Man the levees, boys," C.J. had drawled, "she's gonna blow!"

They had all had a hand in it: C.J. had donated the cigarbox, Jerry had soaked off the labels, sanded, and varnished it, and Bobby had carved her name on the lid. The final *A* was a bit squashed, and the surrounding garland of roses was none too expert, but that did not matter.

"Stop doing The Little Match Girl and open the bloody thing," C.J. had chuckled, and she had whispered, "There's more?" She had thumbed open the catch, lifted the lid—and the world had reeled. Mary had lined the box with flowered cambric; Dulcie had contributed the contents, all tied in place with tiny green ribbons: liquid makeup, eye makeup sticks, pots of lip and cheek rouge, a box of powder and a swansdown puff, squares of toweling to use with the cold cream. There was even a mirror in the lid.

Miranda lay against the pillows, touching each shining treasure in turn. "Maybe," she whispered, "maybe I mean as much to them as they do to me . . . oh, wouldn't it be wonderful if it were true?"

A birthday that was meant to be special from start to finish had to be planned, so every evening that week Miranda and Lucy had walked downtown after supper to buy a New York paper. A day in the City and a matinee was their tradition, but this year the theatrical listings were a disappointment. No Gilbert & Sullivan was playing, and she had seen *Peg O' My Heart* on her last birthday. You could not take a child to the Ziegfeld *Follies*, no matter how hard she begged—and they were most emphatically *not* going to Hammerstein's Roof Garden just so Miranda could get a look at that scandalous Evelyn Nesbit Thaw.

"What about a picture show, Auntie?" This timidly said, with fingers crossed behind her back.

"Hmmm." The thoughtful silence had been excruciating. "I don't see why not, provided it's not in a seedy part of town." Miranda had looked over Lucy's shoulder at the paper, glad her face was hidden while she pretended ignorance of the films listed. C.J. had finally wearied of her incessant questions, and had loaned her copies of *Moving Picture World* and *Photoplay*. He never read anything else. "Who cares if some chinless Archduke shuffles off his mortal coil halfway around the world?" he had once said. "It's certainly not going to affect us."

Lucy had chosen *Quo Vadis*: "It's Roman history, and it'll be

very educational." Well, it was still a real picture show, even if Miranda had had her heart set on *Tess of the Storm Country* with Mary Pickford.

She fidgeted all through breakfast until Lucy took pity on her and said, "You might try the corner of my wardrobe." She replied, "ThankyouverymuchmayIpleasebeexcused," dashed the napkin from her lap, and raced up the back stairs and down the hall, Lucy in amused pursuit. She opened the mirrored doors of the big mahogany wardrobe and leafed quickly through the hanging garments. "But these are all grown-up things, Auntie."

"The one on the end," said Lucy.

"This one? The yellow dress? That's for me?"

Lucy came up behind her, closed the doors, and held the linen dress against the girl. "You're a young lady now, sweetie," she said softly. "I can't keep dressing you like a little girl." She reached up behind the carved pediment over the doors and took down Miranda's Sunday-best straw hat, retrimmed with wide yellow-and-gray striped ribbons to match the dress. She set the hat on Miranda and kissed her cheek. "There, take a look. Very smart."

Miranda turned and hugged her. "Oh, Auntie, you're the best!"

"Darling! You'll wrinkle the dress, and I don't have time to press it again if we're going to catch the ferry. Scoot!"

They walked to the streetcar, Miranda trying not to skip. She was a young lady now, and young ladies did not skip, but the day was like cherry phosphate in her veins. Lucy was not immune either. Her face was calm under her best hat, her hands were calm in spotless kid, the white pleated frills lay calmly, correctly, at the neck and wrists of her navy blue suit, but the expectant staccato of her heels on the sidewalk gave her away.

The luck of Miranda held. They would not reach Fort Lee until midmorning; the hordes of commuting actors would be safely behind studio walls and there would be no risk of running into the McGills. They got off at Main Street, and changed for the trolley

that zigzagged a heart-stopping track down the sheer face of the Palisades to the ferry docks. Miranda pressed her nose to the window; Lucy shut her eyes.

Miranda always insisted upon standing at the very front of the ferry, eyes on distant horizons and uncharted shores. Today there was no need to pretend she was a great explorer. To see the sun on the Hudson, to feel the sturdy boat chopping through the waves, to hear the gulls cawing madly overhead as Manhattan drew near— that was enough.

The ferry docked at 125th Street and Lucy said, "How would you like to go downtown, darling? Shall we splurge on a taxicab?" It was an old game and the answer was always the same. "The subway, Auntie, please." They disembarked and crossed the open plaza to the entrance. Miranda bounded up the escalator to the station; Auntie claimed the whole point of a moving staircase was that it moved so you didn't have to, but what fun was that?

The station was perched midair, for the line through the upper reaches of the West Side was elevated. The train pulled in and they got on, settling back on the shiny wicker-patterned seats (just wide enough for two), watching the motorcars and horse-drawn drays flick under the trestles, counting cats on windowsills, snatching glimpses of the river at cross streets. Then, with a great screeching *whoosh*! the train slid down, down under the city. That was the best part of the trip; half night, half noon, the inky blackness of the tunnel giving onto the bustle of the stations, each decorated with terra-cotta friezes of blue and ocher, carmine and gold, and lit by electric globes high in the curved ceilings. "It's so clean and cool down here," Lucy commented. "Such a modern way to travel."

The train snaked under Broadway to Times Square, then dog-legged over to the year-old Grand Central Terminal. They ascended into the energetic granite vastness of the Main Concourse, craning their necks to admire the constellations twinkling across the ceiling vaulted four stories above, then went out into the hectic glare of 42nd Street.

Lucy checked the locket watch pinned to her jacket and stepped to the edge of the curb. She peered up at the roof, where the mighty bronze clock ticked stoically amid a torment of Classical statuary, and announced: "Eleven-twenty on the button. One hour of shopping—that's all, I promise—then a walk up Fifth for a light luncheon, then the picture show."

Miranda grabbed her arm. "Up Fifth? You mean?"

"Well, it is your birthday, and I knew I could bribe you into shopping if I dangled the Plaza Hotel in front of your nose."

A walk along Fifth Avenue was always exciting, even if Auntie did want to stop in every store: first a sale on clocked hose at Peck & Peck's , then a sale on French Eponge suiting (whatever that was) at McCreery's, then into the enormous B. Altman's, where Auntie looked at every . . . single . . . new . . . fall . . . dress. To the sighs and foot-shifting she replied, "It's part of my job, darling. I have to be up on all the latest styles."

As far as Miranda was concerned the only store in New York worth the trip was Abercrombie & Fitch, over on Madison Avenue. You could play besieged pioneer in the honest-to-goodness log cabin on the roof, and when that paled you could go outside and watch the sporting gentlemen practice fly-casting into the water tank. Mr. Stowing had taken her and Tommy there once on his day off, and they had even seen Teddy Roosevelt "bully"-ing all over the luggage department.

"Miranda, slow down! You'll knock someone over." Shopping completed, they were walking past the limestone châteaux lining Fifth Avenue in the Fifties. It was the Loire Valley disassembled and set in a row; fronted, not by acres of greenery and vineyards, but by sad grass corseted with iron fencing. "And be quiet," she added. "People live here, even if the houses do all look like banks."

A stout gentleman strolling by overheard, smiled as he tipped his homburg, and said, "Astute observation, Madam. That is exactly what they are."

"Now look what you made me do," Lucy moaned when the

man had passed. "That was probably one of the Vanderbilts."

Miranda had slowed down by the time they reached the Plaza. She felt very elegant and mature when the doorman held the door for them, and wished her new dress had a train to it so she could sweep into the Tea Room. It was a hot day, and she was thirsty from walking, but she ordered hot chocolate with her finger sandwiches. The mustachioed waiter bowed gravely over his napkined arm and said, "As Mademoiselle wishes. One *pot du chocolat.*"

"I just like those fat silver pots," she explained. "I can have sarsaparilla or lemonade anytime, an' they give you 'bout four cups here."

The Tea Room at the Plaza Hotel was very like a discreet forest, with the genteel chatter of muted voices and the muffled clinking of silver on china replacing animal calls and birdsong. The air was heavy with the mingled aromas of perfume and pastries and coffee. At the piano, hidden behind stands of ferns, a violinist was sawing through the whipped cream of Kreisler's "Caprice Viennoise." There was so much to look at—the massive pink marble columns, the stained-glass dome, the potted palms banked against the French doors—and the New Yorkers were always interesting.

Lucy pinched her under the little marble table and hissed, "Stop staring at that woman, it's rude."

"But she just ate six cream puffs," Miranda hissed back. "I counted."

"Stop staring right now or there'll be no picture show!"

Miranda stopped staring.

There wasn't time to walk all the way to the theater; they took a double-decker bus back down Fifth, sitting upstairs to cool off, then walked through the theater district. The Astor Theatre was at the northwest corner of Broadway and 45th Street. As they waited for the traffic to clear, Miranda looked across the street and saw the marquee. If Lucy had released her hand at that moment, she knew she would have floated up and over the street like the

thinnest soap bubble. Not even the four cups of chocolate and the two plates of sandwiches would have anchored her.

The tickets were twenty-five cents or fifty cents. "In for a penny, in for a pound," Lucy said gaily to the cashier. "Two of your best orchestra seats, please."

"This looks like the inside of any old theater," Miranda said with a tinge of disappointment. "Same old carpet, same old mirrors and gold gobbledygook."

"What did you expect, darling?" Lucy laughed. "A brass band?"

The usher at the doors into the auditorium smiled at Miranda's expression, winked at Lucy, and escorted them down the center aisle.

The lights dimmed, and the buzz of anticipation filled the theater. A plump man clutching a bulging folder hurried down the side aisle, and over to the musicians gathered in front of the stage. They were a small group, more dance band than orchestra, officiously thumbing through their scores and fussing with bows and pegs and spit valves. (Miranda was reminded of Jerry's early-morning routine with Baby.) The conductor leaned on the podium, cleaning his fingernails with the end of his baton. The pianist slouched over the upright took a furtive sip from a teacup, and hit concert *A*. The thrilling, slovenly dissonance of tuning up began, and Miranda and Lucy exchanged excited glances.

The man handed the folder to the conductor, who distributed the contents with a resigned shrug. The man disappeared through a side door, then reappeared from the wings and crossed to center stage. He held up his hands.

"Folks, uh, folks," he called nervously. The pianist hit a chord ("That thing could use a good tuning," Lucy muttered), and the drummer crashed the cymbal. The whispering abated.

"Folks, uh, welcome to the Astor. We've uh—oh, dear." He wiped his hands on his jacket, leaving damp streaks. "We had a little accident last night during the last show. We, uh, well, we had

a fire. Ya might say Rome burned and then some, heh-heh." The whispers became murmurs, and the manager put his hands up again. "Everything's jake, folks—no one was hurt—but the last reel of *Quo Vadis* ain't fit for mandolin picks. Hey! Settle down! You're gonna get a picture. Nipped down to The Exchange this morning and picked up a new feature to fill the gap. We think it's a real darb, and you regular picturegoers'll recognize the leading lady from her Biograph days. So sit back and enjoy the show. If you want your money back after the show stop by the box office" he said in one breath, and scuttled for the wings.

"Do you want to stay, darling?" Lucy said. The lights were lowered until only the exit lamps were visible, and the curtain over the screen parted. "You bet," Miranda replied in a whisper. "Any picture's fine with me."

The conductor rapped his baton on the podium and raised it; the musicians lifted their instruments and came to attention, eyes shifting between scores and leader. The baton fell.

"That's 'When You Were Sweet Sixteen,' " Lucy whispered. "I love that old song." The woman behind them tapped Lucy on the shoulder and "shushed" impatiently. The orchestra segued, raggedly, into the bittersweet drag of Joplin's "Bethena." It's just coincidence, Miranda thought uneasily. They probably use the same music for all the picture shows.

The harsh beam of the projector slanted down from a small glass window high in the rear wall of the balcony. The opening title appeared:

The American Moving Picture Company
Presents

"Oh, please God," Miranda breathed. "Oh, please let it be something they did before, oh please."

A Drama of Gentle Romance and Gentler Comedy

Miranda looked to one side, then the other. She was between Lucy and a large woman fishing caramels from a paper sack. There was no escape.

Cupid and The Little Sister

"I'm doomed," she whispered. "My life is over. I'm going to die on my birthday."

Lucy leaned over and hissed, "Hush, honey. Be quiet."

Miranda could barely hear through the roaring in her ears. Her hands and feet were tingling, and for one terrible moment she couldn't decide if she wanted to faint or be sick. The polite applause at the cast credits died away, and the picture started. I might as well enjoy the last few minutes of my life, she thought dully. It's my first time at a picture show . . . my last, too, I'll bet. Slowly, fearfully, she lifted her eyes to the screen.

Dulcie and Bobby sat on the porch, as they had when she had spied from her tree, as they had when she had seen the dailies projected on the bedroom wall that first evening, as they had the morning C.J. had run the rough cut—but this! This was something altogether different.

What had been black and white on a painted wall had diffused into gauzy silver. The tint baths had been worth every foul-smelling drop, for The Boy and The Girl were suffused with a warm romantic glow somewhere between peach and amber. The backlit halo around Dulcie's face ("Light her the way Bitzer lights the Gishes, Donnelly") was a luminous, delicate gold. Her rag-set curls shone softly over eyes limpid and liquid and melting. And Bobby! The glued-on mustache he loathed so was masculine and sharp against the pale high cheekbones, and the look in his eyes as he gazed at Dulcie was shy and bold all at once.

Maybe it's because it's so big, thought Miranda, or maybe— Oh, who knows why? Who cares? It's magic, that's all, pure magic. She sighed, and stared spellbound at the faces on the "silversheet"; once

friends, now the mysterious courtiers of a realm as enchanted and faraway as The Kingdom by the Sea.

Lucy leaned over and, without taking her eyes from the screen, whispered, "What a charming couple. She looks familiar, but I can't for the life of me think why"—and Miranda went cold.

"I should have done something," she said later. "But I just couldn't move." She was powerless, held captive by the story unwinding into the light. She knew every shot, she knew every title, but as Bobby and Dulcie had become foreign so had the picture. She despaired over The Father's maniacal hatred (Was that dour giant really Jerry?), and ached for The Boy and The Girl. With open mouth and brimming eyes she watched them walk hand in hand down country lanes, and drift across sun-drenched meadows spangled with daisies, a field of stars at their knees.

"Beyond the human eye into the human heart." That was what C.J. had said. "You'll see," he had whispered, the holy cause illuming his face . . . and now she did. It wasn't only the images. It was the music—oh! the music added so much, even from twenty unrehearsed players—and the safe, anonymous dark of the theater. They were "travelers on the same voyage," everyone around her breathing, reacting, feeling, living the story as one.

They were back to the front porch again, The Boy and The Girl in radiant close-up. Miranda's fear was gone, swept downstream in a buoyant, enfolding current of emotion. Then the branch over Dulcie's head shook, again as always; and her panic returned with the crystal sharpness of the icicles that grew down from the eaves each winter. *She was in trouble.*

She glanced at Lucy; she was having a fine time, lips parted, cheeks rosy with excitement. Oh, Auntie, she thought, enjoy it while you can, 'cause in a minute it'll all be over.

The Little Sister rolled her clumsy crashing way down onto the startled lovers and laughter rocked the theater. Lucy bent low over her knees and gasped, "Oh, how funny! Where did that silly little girl come from?"

Next door, Auntie, next door.

Now Miranda was not watching the screen. She was watching Lucy, staring at the happy face with a dreadful kind of fascination. Lucy was laughing: laughing at the little girl in the pinafore; laughing at the dash down from the porch; laughing at The Girl's tears; laughing at The Boy, checking for broken bones; laughing at The Little Sister chomping down on The Boy's hand; laughing as hard as Miranda had ever seen her laugh; laughing until The Little Sister's face filled the screen in the wickedly grinning close-up—and the laughter stopped.

The color drained from Lucy's face. She looked at the white-faced girl beside her, then at the screen, then at the girl, and her eyes grew as wide as The Little Sister's. *"You!"* she hissed on an intake of breath. "You little liar. No wonder. No wonder you've been so sweet lately. I could just—" Her mouth drew into a line and her jaw set. She bent down and picked up the packages at her feet, then grabbed Miranda by the wrist. "We . . . are . . . go-ing . . . home."

She yanked Miranda out of her seat and dragged her up the aisle. Behind them the theater was filled with gasps, muttered comments, and (from several impressionable young women) screams as "The Boy fought—like one possessed!—to save The Little Sister from a cruel Death in the cold embrace of the River."

Out of the theater they fled, rushing through the deserted lobby past the ushers draped bored against the stairs to the balcony. Lucy banged the street door open with her hip and pulled Miranda out onto the sidewalk.

They scurried through the lamplit dusk, Lucy's viselike grip unrelenting. Stumbling, running, they made their way along the crowded sidewalks until Lucy spotted a subway kiosk and jerked Miranda through the glass pagoda and down the stairs. The trip uptown was made in strained silence, the morning's excitement gone now in a gloomy tunnel and a noisy train. Down from the station and into the ferry terminal they marched, Lucy snapping

open her handbag and shoving money abruptly at the startled ticket seller.

They walked, Lucy's head up, Miranda's head down, to the stern of the boat. Lucy dumped her packages on the slatted wooden seat and dropped down beside them. She flung Miranda's hand away angrily, folded her arms over her waist, and turned to stare out over the river. Miranda sat several feet away, and stole sideways peeks at the stony face.

Once, and only once, did Lucy speak during the long trip home. The ferry was midway through its journey to the landing nestled at the foot of the Palisades, and the lights of the great city were receding against the last frail warmth of the sunset.

"Oh, Auntie," Lucy said, her mocking voice pitched high. "Nothing ever happens to me." She looked over at Miranda. "Hah!"

The Widow's Revenge

Just before dawn Miranda slid out of bed, draped her quilt around her shoulders, and padded over to the window seat. I want my SueSue, said the sad voice in her head.

She lifted the cushioned lid and reached into the toy box underneath, fumbling past the abandoned dolls and discarded games until she found the grimy wad of chintz. From Lucy's ragbag SueSue had come, and to rag she had returned. Little remained of the doll, made to console a small girl who sat with frightened eyes outside the room where her Mama and Papa lay dying. "Oh, SueSue," Miranda whispered, "I been bad."

She closed the lid, wrapped close the quilt as much for comfort as warmth, and curled up in the corner of the window seat with SueSue pressed in the hollow of her neck. I can't even cry, she thought. I'm all cold and dead, like Bobby's voice when he talks about his mother. . . . She wanted to cry, she needed to cry, for only crying would ease the terrible tightness in her chest, but this was too big for tears.

In the filmy half-light before sunrise the houses were barely visible, the trees dark shapes against a charcoal sky. Miranda rested her head against the window frame, and watched the house next door. The old Macdougall place . . . just a shabby house on a quiet street on the east side of a small town in the Jersey woods, but there lived magic.

Maybe I'll have to go to boarding school, she thought, and live in an attic and wear one dress all the time like Sara Crewe. "No," she whispered. "I know what'll happen. They'll go away and I'll never see them again, and that'll be worse punishment than being locked in my room forever or getting sent to the county orphanage." She spoke the hallowed names slowly, saving the best for last: "C.J. . . . Jerry . . . Mary . . . Dulcie . . . Bobby. My best friend."

When Lucy opened the bedroom door the birds were shrilling their coloratura chorus in the treetops, and the sun was up. Miranda was still huddled at the window, a brightly quilted heap of misery. "Get dressed," said Lucy. "After breakfast we're going next door. I intend to get to the bottom of this, one way or another."

Miss Lucy Gaines and her niece walked out their front door, across the front porch, down the brick walk to the sidewalk, along the sidewalk past the drive, and up to the front door of the Macdougall house. Miranda thought of The Boy walking to the waiting noose, and wondered if Bobby'd had the same sick lump under his ribs. She peeked at Lucy's face, shadowed by the wide brim of her second-best summer straw.

Lucy said, quite unexpectedly, "Butterflies in your stomach?" Miranda nodded.

"I should think so," said Lucy. She smoothed her skirt over her hips, and turned the doorbell. They heard the grinding ring echo in the empty hallway, but no one came. Lucy cranked the bell again. Still no answer. She knocked on the door with a gloved fist and it swung ajar.

C.J. strode down the hall. A napkin was tucked in his open collar and he carried a piece of toast, tearing off bites as he grouched, "What're you waiting for, Madame? An engraved invitation on Tif-

fany stock? Just barge in—" Lucy pushed the door open. He crammed in the last of the toast and whipped the napkin into his pocket. "A thousand pardons, my dears. Thought you were Black Bess. Who have we here, Missy?"

"Good morning," Lucy said crisply, and extended her hand. "I am Miss Gaines, Miss Lucinda Gaines. This child's aunt."

C.J. took Lucy's hand, but instead of shaking it he bowed low and kissed it, clicking his heels with Prussian smartness: Not for nothing had he played *The Student Prince* in stock.

"This?" he said, suavely cocking an eyebrow. "This fashion plate is the decrepit old auntie you're always bemoaning? She looks in the pink to me. As a matter of fact," he mused, casting a practiced eye, "she is altogether most presentable. My dear young woman, I am Charles James Tour—"

Miranda could bear no more. She ducked under the clasped hands and headed for the back of the house. C.J. was in top form, Lucy his blushing captive. "—otherwise known to all and sundry as C.J., the—" On she ran, down the hall and through the kitchen door, homing for high ground.

Bobby was standing at the sink. "Hey, Red." He grinned his crooked grin—and she flung herself across the room at him, sending them both crashing against the drainboard. He grabbed her shoulders and started to laugh; then he saw her face, and the teasing died on his lips. "What's wrong?" he said gently. "You look rotten, kid."

"Jig's up," she whispered tensely. "Auntie's talkin' to C.J. right now. What'm I gonna do?"

"She hopping mad?" he asked. Before Miranda could answer Jerry said from across the room, "What's up wit' you two?"

"Nothin'," Bobby said quickly. "Whatever happens act like it's a normal morning, okay?"

"Doors slamming, drama over breakfast," Mary said mildly. "Sounds like business as usual."

Bobby bent down and peered into Miranda's face. "Let me do

the talkin'; I can read C.J. better'n you," he said in a low voice. "Play it pathetic and follow my lead. Start bawlin'."

Miranda shook her head. "Can't," she whispered. "Gone dry."

"Whaddya mean?" he hissed. "Fine time you picked. Well, fake it. Act like an orphan, for cryin' out lou—quick, they're comin'!" He grabbed her and pulled her onto his shirtfront.

"Can't breathe," Miranda said in a strangled voice.

"Quit gripin'," he muttered, and loosened his hold. "An' start sobbin'." He patted her awkwardly on the back and said loudly, "Oh, Miranda, it'll be all right, it'll be all right."

"That's what you think!" C.J. said in the doorway, Lucy at his side. "It seems Little Miss Sneaky Pete has been acting up the proverbial storm offscreen as well as on."

"Speak plain, Boss," said Jerry. "Just once, to see how y' like it."

The director flung an arm straight at Miranda and took a deep breath. "Not only did that—that vest-pocket Duse," he thundered, "not have permission to be in our picture, she was expressly forbidden to come anywhere near this house. Or us!" He turned to the open-mouthed Donnellys. "This is Lucinda Gaines," he explained, "the long-suffering aunt. She has just spilled the beans on Missy here. Apparently that Duncan dreadnought organized a ban on this place—a feeble attempt at keeping their lily-white brats out of our clutches." He started to chuckle, then remembered his anger. "Ye gods! Fond as I am of the obstreperous little midget, I would never have—"

"Stop it, Boss," Bobby cut him off. He shoved Miranda to one side and squared his shoulders. "Please. I gave her the responsibility speech weeks ago."

"You knew?" C.J.'s eyes bulged. "God in heaven, boy, why didn't you say something?"

"We'd shot half the picture by then," Bobby said simply. He looked around at the astonished faces, his eyes coming to rest on

the most astonished of all. "She's part of the Company, Boss. She's part of us. And she's been walking a tightrope all summer, so don't be too hard on her." He nudged Miranda.

Miranda buried her face in her hands and "boo-hooed" purposefully. "Don't overplay it," Bobby murmured. She turned down the volume, and peeked dry-eyed between her fingers.

"Well!" said C.J. He pulled out the napkin and wiped his forehead, leaving a track of breadcrumbs across the shiny surface, then balled it up and threw it to the floor. "Not only have I been lied to, now I am to be lectured to?"

"Wait just a minute," said Lucy. She turned and laid a hand on C.J.'s arm. "Do you mean that you didn't know that I didn't know that—oh, for heaven's sake. Let me get this straight. I didn't know my niece was in your flicker—"

"Moving picture," five voices corrected.

"Pardon me! Your moving picture. And none of you knew she was lying to you as well? No one except that fellow?" She pointed at Bobby.

"That is the Leading Man of my Company," C.J. glowered, "and he had better talk fast if he wants to—"

"Wait, wait!" Lucy said. Miranda ground her knuckles into her eyes and thought dimly, Auntie never interrupts like that.

Lucy squinted nearsightedly at Bobby, then took her spectacles out of her bag and hooked them on. "He's the one from the picture show! Why, he's only a boy."

"I'm Robert Gilmer, Miss Gaines, but please call me Bobby. You don't know how sorry I am 'bout all this. Honestly, Miranda and I didn't want to lie to you—or anyone else, Boss—but she was already in the picture, and doin' swell. Yes, ma'am," he said sheepishly, "that was me. A little greasepaint, a little mus— *You saw the picture? Where?*"

"In the City," Lucy answered absently, eyes narrowed as she tried to connect the gangling youth with the lean, mustached hero of the silversheet. "At the Astor Theatre. It's at Broadway—"

"I know where it is!" Bobby blurted, his grin fairly splitting his face. "The Astor? We're playin' the Astor? That's big time!" He punched Miranda's shoulder. "Hey, we're playin' the Astor!" He glared at C.J. and said, "Why dincha tell us, Boss?"

"A little surprise I was saving 'til after breakfast, dear boy. Spot booking at yesterday's matinee. Got a call from The Exchange late last night." He smiled with irritating blandness.

"I know y' like to bleed a good line," Jerry groaned, "but so help me."

"They liked it," C.J. said smugly. "Very much. The Astor wants to put it on at matinees, and The Exchange already has some orders lined up. Brooklyn, Queens—Timbuktu, for all I care!" He opened his arms as if to embrace them all. "We're on our way, my children. The worst is over!"

With raised hands he quelled the congratulatory babble: "We cannot let this most golden of opportunities flit by. We have, in Miss Lucinda here, our public. Audience reaction! The final arbiter of our blood-soaked tribulations." He took Lucy's hands and, looking directly into her eyes, said, "It is a fine film, I must say, as who shouldn't. How about that finale? Tore your heart out, didn't it? The depth of emotion! The pathos! The—what's the matter? Where are my manners? Mistress Donnelly, some libations for our guest, if you please."

Mary got up from the table, crossed to the doorway, and shepherded Lucy to a chair. "You just sit there and I'll fix you a cup of tea." She glanced at C.J., then said quietly, "And don't mind him, dearie. Swallowed a dictionary backwards, he did. Good-hearted, though," and she bustled over to the stove, giving a swift, motherly kiss to Miranda's cheek as she passed.

Lucy leaned her elbows on the table (another breach of etiquette, Miranda noticed), and said in a dazed voice, "I do not understand all this commotion. Films, bookings, pathos. . . ." She took her handkerchief from her sleeve, cleaned her spectacles, and stared at C.J.; he seemed very pleased with himself. "I do not un-

derstand," she repeated. "I thought we were discussing Miranda. I could cheerfully murder her this very minute—and I should think you would all feel the same."

"Life's too short," Jerry said gravely, "fer tryin' to change what can't be changed. Spilt milk, as me mum used t' say."

"But don't you realize what she's done? What you've done?" Lucy persisted. "I could take you to court if I wanted to, Mr. Tourneur. Kidnapping, or corrupting the morals of a minor. And I'm sure The Gerry Society would have something to say."

"If?" Miranda exchanged glances with Bobby, who gave her a discreet thumbs-up signal.

C.J. flung the tails of his scarf over his shoulder. "Once more unto the breach," he said under his breath, and turned on the full wattage of his charm. "It's over and done with, my dear Miss Lucinda," he said warmly. "It's a *fait accompli*. The Gerry Society'd be powerless; she's past the cut-off age for their ridiculous strictures. As it was, the work was neither taxing nor the hours long. And I give you my word we do not go rampaging through godforsaken hamlets looking for little girls to corrupt." His eyes twinkled mischievously. "As for kidnapping, 'twas merest happenstance. She fell out of a tree smack-dab into—"

"I've told her not to climb trees," Lucy whimpered. "Time and time again I've told her, but does she listen to me?" Jerry clucked sympathetically and reached over to pat her hand.

"—the scene we were shooting. Once we had ascertained that the wench hadn't broken her neck, and checked the footage, it seemed natural enough to include her. She films well, actually, and has a somewhat energetic quality that—"

He really has the bit in his teeth now, thought Miranda. She wiped her nose on her sleeve and prayed: Oh, Boss, wonderful Boss, just keep on talking. Bamboozle Auntie the way you did me the very first day.

"—reminds me of a young Dorothy Gish. Well I remember the

day she and the delectable Lillian first came to Fourteenth Street, and D.W. chased the poor lambs all over the set firing a revol—" He pulled up short; not the most appropriate anecdote, perhaps, given the situation. "I refer, Lucinda, to The American Biograph and Mutoscope Company. In its hallowed and somewhat dusty halls we all learned our trade, and there is no finer training for the moving picture game. But, as I was saying, Miranda has—"

Mary placed a cup of tea in front of Lucy, wiped her hands on her apron, and started to clear the breakfast dishes. Jerry lit his pipe and settled back in his chair. Ah! the old days. How he loved to hear C.J. ramble on in that rich voice, tellin' tales, spinnin' yarns.

"—an engaging comedic touch. Now, I don't want to give the impression that I condone the child's duplicity, but I cannot honestly say that I blame her. My one regret is that the, ah—shall we say narrow-mindedness?—of the local climate forced her to pursue a burgeoning career incognito, and that you, Lucinda dear, have been denied the pleasure of—"

The front door slammed with a loud report, awakening them from the hypnotic caress of The Voice. Footsteps skittered down the hall. "Charlie, oh, Charlie-e-e-ee!"

The Leading Lady of The American Moving Picture Company made her entrance. Her eyes were wide with fear. Windblown tendrils framed a face as white as her fragile summer frock, and the lace-trimmed square between her trembling hands was shredded to a ruin. The effect was not unbecoming. She grabbed the doorjamb for support, and her face crumpled with anguish. "Oh, Charlie-ee," she wailed, and pressed a dainty fist to her lips.

C.J. stopped mid-soliloquy, pivoted, and put a hand to his chest. "My Sweet! My Pet! What gives?"

Dulcie stretched an arm out to him, hand back and slightly curled, and averted her face. "No, no, My Darling, I cannot face you. Such shame as mine cannot be borne. My despair is utter!"

"My stomach is turning," Bobby muttered.

"Dulcinea! Get ahold of yourself," C.J. said, taking the outstretched hand in his. "You are splendid in your turmoil, but what in blue blazes is going on?"

The big eyes filled with tears. "She did it. Mamma. She's out in the hall waiting for the fireworks. She's been so sweet lately I knew something was wrong. I finally wormed it out of her on the ferry." She bit a knuckle and hiccuped delicately.

"What did she do, My Little Crumbcake?" C.J. crooned. "Try to marry you off to some pimpled pinhead?" The blond curls shook back and forth. "Sell your contract to that twit Cecil DeMille?" The curls danced again. "What, then?"

The broken whisper dropped into the sunny room with the resonance of stones down a well. "She called Al McCoy."

"WHAT?"

"That's torn it," Jerry said flatly.

"Dulcie!" gasped Miranda. "Not McCoy!"

"We're finished," Bobby said. "Finished."

"The Astor?" Miranda said hopefully. "Bobby, what about the Astor?" She shook his arm; no answer. "Jerry? They can't hurt us if *Cupid*'s already in a theater, can they?"

"Oh, can't they," he said heavily. "One print out there don't mean spit. They'll find it, seize it . . . ain't important. If they get Baby 'n' the master we're deader'n a mackerel."

"It's all tied up in *Cupid*, Miranda," Bobby said. "Every red cent. Besides," he said woodenly, "remember Pinnacle? McCoy'll run us through. We're done for. Oh, Boss, you never shoulda kissed her."

"Would somebody please tell me," Lucy said plaintively, "what you're all talking about? Who is this McCoy person?"

"Only the biggest goon on the East Coast," Miranda said officiously. "Him and his two plug-uglies from—" She barely had time to notice the startled expression on Lucy's face when Bobby grabbed her and hissed, "Quick! Lookit the Boss!"

C.J. was staring at the doorway and smiling a wide, deadly smile.

There was a marbled look to his skin and his nostrils were flared. "Called McCoy, she did," he said softly. "Oh, did she. Indeed. Indeed. O-o-o-oh Bessie my dear—come here for a minute, will you?" Breaths were held. "Come into the garden, Bessie," oozed the calm, syrupy voice. "We won't hurt you, Bessie dear. We just want to talk to you. . . ."

The Widow put her head around the edge of the door.

"Oh, that she dares to show her face," Mary breathed, and Jerry trapped her hands between his and held them tight. He got up from the table and stood beside her; the Donnellys against the Trust, the Donnellys against the world.

"What have you done, Bessie?" C.J. continued in a queer, honeyed voice that sent shivers up Miranda's spine. "Don't like us anymore, do you? Called the Trust down on me, did you?" He curled his hands into fists, the sinews in his forearms knotting ominously. The linoleum creaked as his weight shifted.

Jerry's eyes widened in alarm. "Get 'im, Rob!" he yelled, and sprang across the room. Bobby ran for C.J.; they reached the director at the same time. "You get one arm, I'll get the other," Jerry gasped. Bobby braced against the stove and hung on like a terrier pup with a slipper.

Mary pulled Lucy from her chair—her hat went flying—and dragged her across the room. "Gimme a hand. He's gonna kill her and I just washed that floor." She grabbed Jerry's waist, and Lucy, after a questioning look, grabbed Bobby. The tug-o'-war held.

C.J.'s face was a bright unhealthy pink. The Voice had returned, booming with fulsome clarity and terrifyingly moist consonants. "Thou cream-faced loon!" he sprayed, a tiny muscle at the corner of one eye jumping. "Troll! Cow! How you ever spawned My Dulcinea! Get me my gallows, we'll lynch the scrag!"

Bessie had the grace—or the common sense—to look afraid, but she stood her ground, victory in her pale eyes. The litany of anger and betrayal raged: "She-devil! Medusa! Festering wound! Calumnious besom!"

The Widow's Revenge

"Calm down, willya?" Jerry yelled. "This ain't gonna help us none!"

C.J. pulled against his restraints like a thoroughbred eager for the starting gate. "Just once, Donnelly," he bawled. "Lemme hit 'er just once."

"Y' know y' never hit a woman in yer life," Jerry panted.

"That's no woman!" he howled. "That's Judas Iscariot in a corset! *Lemme at 'er!*"

I wonder . . . thought Miranda. Sleeve-tugging was going to get her nowhere. She darted across the room and climbed onto the table. It rocked unevenly; she crouched until she got her sea legs, then stood. She closed her eyes, took a deep breath—and screamed.

Miranda opened her eyes, and almost laughed. The frozen tableau looked exactly like a production still from one of the Boss's picture magazines. The Widow was backed against the hutch, her rolling eyes and flower-bedecked hat giving her the appearance of a spooked cart horse; C.J. was strained forward against Jerry and Bobby, his mouth agape; Dulcie was fastened desperately around C.J.'s neck, golden locks streaming down her back. Mary and Lucy brought up the rear, cabooses on a very odd train.

"I think I know—" Miranda choked. She swallowed and started again. "I have an idea."

Baby Takes a Trip

Miranda was not sure it was the best idea she had ever had—it wasn't up there with switching the labels on the canned goods in Old Lady Duncan's pantry—but it was, at the very least, constructive. C.J.'s idea had been more direct. A year of prospecting for Mexican gold had left him with a distaste for his own cooking, a loathing for the humble burro—and a revolver. The trusty Colt was still at the bottom of his trunk, and there was a clear shot at the front walk from the parlor windows. Jerry had scotched that one: "If I ain't gonna let y' hit no one, I ain't gonna let y' murder no one. Not even that weasel McCoy."

It was going to be a tight squeeze, but if everyone pitched in and they rounded up a few more hands. . . . "The Irregulars!" Bobby cried—and they were out the back door.

Hand in hand they raced down the path to the Matawan, Miranda more airborne than earthbound in her attempt to match Bobby's long-legged loping. At The Little Sister's clearing they turned and ran along the river's edge, leaping from stone to fallen log with the surefootedness of mountain goats. They reached the best fort Leewood Heights had ever seen, thrashed through the tangled willow curtain, and burst into the clearing. "You gotta help us!"

Tommy looked up from his cards, and blew a lazy oval of smoke. "Thought that was you comin'. Where's the fire?"

Jimmy frowned at his hand; no face cards. "Geemunittly, I hate this game."

Miranda stumbled over to Tommy and grabbed his arm. "Now!" she panted. "There's no time if we're gonna move it all; they'll be here at noon."

"But I jus' raised," Tommy said, dumbfounded; what was wrong with her? She knew poker was sacred.

The door was not going to open with bludgeoning, but Bobby had the key. "There's gonna be a raid," he said, voice throbbing with the promise of bloodshed. "A detective's coming to try to shut down the Company. An' he'll probably have his goons along. We need every hand we can get, and we can trust you. You can help us foil 'em."

"We gotta move all the picture things over to my house," Miranda said impatiently and shook Tommy's arm again; the cards went flying. "It's a matter of life and death!"

"Listen," Bobby said, "if you help us out we'll show you something you're not supposed to see."

"Like what?" said Jimmy, unmoved. "You already showed us them movin' pitcher magazines with the wimmen in 'em."

"Oh, nothing much," he said blithely. "Just your mother in a moving picture."

"Aw, yer nuts," said Jimmy. "She don't even like to sing in church. What'd she be doin' in a pitcher show?"

"Oh, nothing much," echoed Miranda, eyes locked with Bobby's in mutual congratulation. "Just beatin' the tar outta me on the back of the streetcar."

Tommy looked skeptically at Miranda, then Bobby. "For free?

We don't gotta pay?" Bobby smiled casually and shook his head. The light of commerce glinted in Tommy's eyes. "Sa-a-a-ay," he said slowly, "my dad'd pay a dime to see that."

"Are you kiddin'?" croaked Jimmy. "My dad'd pay a dollar!"

With invisible banners flying, Miranda headed up the procession to her house, winding across the yard and up the back stairs to the attic: first came Jerry, Baby swaddled snug on his shoulder in her bunting of army green, then Bobby and The Pine Street Irregulars, arms stacked to the chin with cans of *Cupid and the Little Sister.* Baby was hidden behind trunks and boxes so not even the tips of her legs showed, and space was cleared on the floor for the prints. "Stack 'em square, boys," Jerry said. "We'll tarp 'em so's it looks like a big box." He gave his darlin' a final pat, and it was down the ladder for the second trip, and the third, and the fourth.

Mary and Lucy hurriedly converted the tiny bedroom off the kitchen into a sewing room. "Easier than moving it all," Mary said, busily buttoning clothing over the two mannequins. Lucy was putting up fashion plates from her collection of *Ladies' Home Journals*, Bobby's pictures of cowboy stars Tom Mix and William S. Hart torn down and hidden under the cot.

The projection room had been stripped of equipment, tar paper, and chairs (there were now eight crammed around the kitchen table), and the dismantling of the laboratory was in progress. The drying drum had been easier than first thought; one end pried free and the spokes had fallen with a great clatter, to be gathered up like so many broomsticks. Dulcie cleared the worktable, her destination the back bedroom next to Miranda's; only Baby and *Cupid* needed the supreme sanctuary of the attic.

The Widow sat in the kitchen and observed the chaos with her usual good humor. After C.J. had been peeled off her, her fate had been discussed. Miranda had wanted to lock her in the cellar, and had been disappointed to learn there were no rats. "Rats?" C.J. had bellowed. "Who needs rats? We have *her!*" In the end all sugges-

tions of violence, however gratifying, had been tabled in deference to the shamefaced Dulcie, and Bessie had been shoved into a chair and left to stew. "It won't do you any good," she stated from time to time. "None of it."

Jerry and C.J. reentered the kitchen, putting scarf and bandana to good use. Unable to face maneuvering the developing vat into another house and up another flight of stairs, they had elected to stow it in the shed at the end of Lucy's vegetable garden. They were very sorry about the windows, and perhaps Miss Gaines could supply the name of a reputable glazier?

Miss Gaines had more pressing concerns than broken glass, namely how to turn a barren barracks into a model of domesticity. Why, the way these people lived was one step above camping out! "Lamps," she said firmly. "Dresser scarves on all the bureaus. Pictures. There's a set of engravings in my front hall that'll dress up the dining room nicely. Oh, Mr. Tourneur, what are all those long glass tubes doing in there?"

C.J. grabbed his head and turned pale. "Good God almighty, we forgot the Cooper-Hewitts! Donnelly—"

"Right-o, Boss. On me way."

"Get Robert and Missy to help, I'll stay here and play house." Jerry opened the screen door and shouted, "Robbie! Red! Front 'n' center!" He headed for the dining room, and C.J. turned his attention to the two women.

"Now, Miss Lucinda," he said, rubbing his hands. "What would lend the proper homey touch? Set the scene, as it were." He gazed at the ceiling for inspiration. "Ah-hah! Lucinda my dear, I understand you have a piano."

"Over my dead body!" Lucy parked fists on hips. "And don't start talking about Mexico and pistols and such. I will help you get through this day—after the pickle Miranda put you in I owe you that much—but hands off my Steinway!"

"What fire!" C.J. chortled. "What spirit! Ah, those Gaines women . . . have you ever considered the stage, my dear?"

Lucy turned an incredulous face to Mary, who shrugged and said, "What did I tell you? Never a dull day."

The Boy, The Girl, and The Little Sister arrived at the back door simultaneously, and there was giggling, wriggling pantomime as they tried to squeeze through. Miranda won, but stopped shrieking when she spotted her aunt. Coolly, Lucy said, "Come, Mary, we'll go get those things," and shouldered her way past.

"Don't fret, Missy," said C.J. "The ice floes are breaking a treat; we'll thaw her out yet. You and Robert go help Donnelly in the dining room. How goes the upstairs, Pet?"

"All done," Dulcie replied. "I think those two little boys have almost all of the prints moved."

"All," Bobby confirmed. "I sent 'em down to the corner to watch for cars." He nudged Miranda and laughed. "Jim's up a tree with binoculars, and Tom's hiding in a bush in his front yard."

C.J. pulled out his watch and scowled at it. "Five of eleven, God help us. Back to work; I want everyone in this kitchen at half-past eleven—sharp—for a final run-through."

The last to make the trip was a plate of minced ham sandwiches, crusts removed, covered with a dampened tea towel. (The Leewood Heights Ladies' Benevolent Society would just have to eat cake.) "Icebox, second shelf. And don't drop that plate, it was your grandmother's," Lucy said as she aimed Miranda out the door with a smack on the backside. Miranda ran—I've been running all day, she thought—and skidded back into the kitchen just as the meeting began.

Parts had been assigned. Dulcie was to play The Wife, although C.J. had said she would look a child bride at best. "Don't worry," she had assured him, "I am an actress, you know." Her costume was so effective he had walked right past her in the hall. Her curls were pulled into a tight bun, Lucy's spectacles adorned a face scrubbed free of powder and rouge, and she wore a dark skirt and a droopy gray cardigan of Jerry's over her lacy frock. "Ye gods!" he

had cried. "I said drab yourself down a bit, not—you look like the grimmest suffragette to ever come down the pike."

The Company got the once-over while C.J. knotted his tie. Five minutes previous he had looked down at his boots and raced upstairs to put on the linen suit; breeches and boots were a dead giveaway if you could not produce a horse. "Hmmm. As boring a bunch of bourgeoisie as I could wish; it'll play. Any word from our sentries, Robert?" Bobby shook his head. "I devoutly hope we haven't forgotten anything." He glanced at Bessie, and groaned, "Oh, yes we have. What are we going to do about Benedict Arnold?"

"There's nothing you can do, you disgusting little man," Bessie sniffed. "None of this will do you a bit of good. I'm going to watch them shut you down—and then I am going to sue you for everything you owe me and more."

"Money?" said Dulcie. "That's why you did this? For money?" She swayed, and for a moment it looked as though she would faint. "I've given you every penny I ever made since I was five, Mamma. I did what you wanted, living in those dreadful boardinghouses and saving it all—and for what? Oh, Mamma," she said in a pained whisper. "Oh, Mamma, how could you."

"Stop acting like a child," The Widow snapped. "That man owes us three weeks' back salary."

"What?" Bobby blurted, and turned to C.J. "Since when is she gettin' paid regular? I thought we all agreed to wait for our money."

Dulcie looked at Bobby's red face, and her eyes widened. "So did I," she said. "I thought we were all in this together." She turned to her mother and said, "This is more of your doing, isn't it. I knew you didn't like him, but so little faith? So little faith in the picture? So little faith in me? We had enough to live on, you didn't have to be so greedy. Charlie needed the money more than we did."

"Oh, My Pet," said C.J. "Calm yourself. This will—"

"How could you, Charlie?" Dulcie said with a kind of despair. "How could you of all people just knuckle under to her?"

For once his words were to the point. "It was the only way I could get you here, dearest. You're not of legal age."

Dulcie exploded. It was a new experience for one trained from birth to a limpid, clinging femininity, but life before the footlights had stiffened her backbone more than she knew. She drew herself proudly to her full five feet and lifted her little chin defiantly. "I have had enough of you, Mamma!" she announced. "This is the end of the line for you. *Your* money? *My* money. You wanna get a job? Do you?" She pointed to her chest. "Me, Mamma. I'm the one. I'm the one who keeps us in room and board and—and those stupid hats of yours. I'll never work again and then you'll starve and see if I care. See if I care, Mamma."

She went to the table and leaned over until her face was inches from The Widow's. "You will do what I say, Mamma, or I will walk out of this house and you will never . . . see . . . me . . . again. Devoting yourself to my career? Pooh. Did you hear me, Mamma? I said pooh. Pooh and phooey and—" She swallowed, and said, *"Blast."* The Widow's lips thinned to a gray line and vanished. Dulcie leaned in and said, *"Bloody* blast. What do you think of that?" Bessie's face showed the disbelief one would exhibit upon seeing a pig tap-dance. Dulcie was beginning to crumble, unshed tears shining in her eyes, but there was one arrow left in the quiver. "And, and, and—"

"Don't quit now," C.J. breathed. "You're almost there."

"And I can too kiss Charlie if I want to!" She turned awkwardly, fell across the space between them, and collapsed, sobbing raucously, into the director's waiting arms.

"Home run," Bobby murmured. "And the crowd goes wild."

"Magnificent!" C.J. crowed. "My plucky little dragon-slayer!" He looked over her head at The Widow, and, to his credit, refrained from gloating. "You heard her," he said curtly. "If you want to keep your tenuous hold on this charming meal-ticket, you will do as she—and I—say." He kissed the top of Dulcie's head and said, "Places, everyone. To the parlor. Come, Wife."

Miranda twitched aside the front window curtains (previously her bedroom curtains), as two heads rose above the windowsill. "There's a car comin'!" Tommy said excitedly. "I seen it! A big black one, comin' from the river."

"Jimmy! Jim-me-e-e-eee!"

"Aw, nuts," Jimmy said. "What's she want now?"

"Get outta here, get outta here," Miranda wailed. "Quick, she can't know you're here."

"Put a lid on that caterwauling," C.J. barked.

"It's Old Lady Duncan," Miranda said over her shoulder. "She's right across the street." She stuck her head out the window and said, "For Pete's sake, do something!"

Tommy whispered into Jimmy's ear; his eyes grew round and he said, "And how!" The two boys ran across the yard and into the middle of the street. Miranda started to laugh.

"What's so funny?" Bobby said from across the room. "What're they doing?"

"Fightin'," said Miranda. "You oughta see it. Tommy just picked up a big handful of dirt and threw it in Jimmy's face . . . now Jimmy's kickin' him . . . uh-oh, here she comes."

"Oh, Miranda," said Lucy. "Get away from that window."

"But it's working," Miranda protested. Through the open window they could hear, over the noise of an approaching automobile, Emma Duncan's piercing voice: "Stop it, stop it . . . Thomas Stowing, you stop that this very minute. Leave him alone, you little bully. Jimmy! Get out of the road, there's a car coming. Stop it! Jimmy! Jimmy!" The voice faded, and they heard the Duncans' front door slam loudly.

"Back to your place, Missy," C.J. ordered. "And—" He was cut off by the doorbell, the tinny ring reverberating with the brassy panic of a fire bell. He strode to the archway into the hall, turned, said, "Let's do it in one, children!" and went to answer the door.

"Pour the tea," Mary whispered to The Widow. The Widow grabbed the handle of Lucy's second-best teapot and poured from

cup to cup in a continuous stream. Lucy snatched a napkin from the tray and mopped hastily. She was on The Widow's left flank, the three women packed into the mangy embrace of a Chesterfield sofa that had once graced the Green Room of the Belasco Theater, or so C.J. claimed. "Miranda, get over here," she whispered loudly. "Pass the sandwiches."

"Oh, Precious," C.J. trilled. "We have visitors." He stood in the doorway and looked back into the hall. "Come and meet the family," he said heartily. "We'll straighten this out."

A slight swarthy man with narrow features slid into the room. He said nothing for a minute, but his eyes shifted rapidly from face to face; taking in, Miranda was sure, every pore. Two hard-bitten–looking men stood behind him. The taller one rocked on the balls of his feet, soundlessly punching an open palm with a closed fist. The other stared at Dulcie; no amount of "drabbing down" could disguise her prettiness.

"Any of you—hold the phone." The sharp-eyed man pulled a folded document from an inside pocket and read off the cover: "Charles James Tower-newer?"

"Mistaken identity," C.J. said, and ran a finger around under his collar. "Case of mistaken identity. The names are so close. Mine is Charles James Turner. That must be—"

"Nope." The infamous Al "Slim" McCoy, Terror of the Independents, cut him off briskly. "No mistake. Had a tip. Same town. Same address. Yer runnin' a picture comp'ny here, Buddy, and it's about as legal as votin' twice."

Mr. Turner was appalled. "A picture company? You mean—? Oh, you couldn't possibly mean—not those dreadful flickers?" He shuddered, but Miranda knew it was because he had demeaned his revered moving pictures.

"Oh, ain't we cultured," said McCoy. He jerked his head at the sofa. "I suppose that's the Queen Mother."

"That, sir, is my wife's mother, Bessie Arnold." He walked over and held out his hand. Mary nudged The Widow, who lifted a hand

reluctantly. C.J. kissed it, glaring meaningfully at her. Miranda was standing behind the sofa so she could see what McCoy could not; a good inch of air separated lips and hand. She heard a faint squeak as Bessie ground her teeth.

C.J. straightened, and gestured, "And this is Miss Lucinda Gaines, a dear friend and a pillar of the community. She and her niece live next door. Say hello to Mr. McCoy, Miranda."

Miranda curtsied and said sweetly, "How do you do, sir." She offered the plate. "Would you like a ham sandwich?"

"Say, girlie," the man said, "are you on the level? Do I want a sandwich."

"And this," C.J. said quickly, "is Mary Donahue. She and her husband Jeremiah are summering with us. Jeremiah is helping me complete my memoirs. Just through the Injah years—"

Slim McCoy threw up his hands. "I didn't come here for no da— pardon me, ladies, no dratted drawin'-room comedy. Cut the introductions, I ain't Mrs. Astor." He turned to the men behind him and snapped, "Turn this dump over. I'll stay in here and give these jokers the third degree." He arched his back and put his hands in his pockets; deliberately, for in brushing aside his jacket he exposed the gun in his waistband. Slowly, with a fiendishly casual air, he strolled around the room.

"Tea, anyone?" Lucy said in a shaky voice; no one responded. With cold hands and dry mouths the Company tracked the heavy footsteps up the stairs, listening as drawers and closet doors began jerking open and slamming shut in a frightening, jagged rhythm.

McCoy stopped in front of Jerry. "Big fer a seccatary, ain't ya."

Jerry stared at him and said nothing. Mary had cut the signature curls off his mustache (he had refused to part with the whole) and parted his hair in the middle, coaxing it into two spit curls over his forehead. A pair of cracked pince-nez had been spirit-gummed to his nose. He was not the Casper Milquetoast desired, but he was neither The Father, The Hangman, nor the former Tannhauser security guard.

McCoy leaned over and stared at him intently; then rapidly barked, "Was you ever at the Biograph?"

"I never was," Jerry said hoarsely. "Ask me wife."

"And how," the man said evenly, "do you know what that is."

"I don't," he said uneasily. "What is it?" There was a screeching sound from overhead as a bedstead was scraped across a bare floor. Jerry started, and grabbed the arms of the chair.

"I know what it is," Dulcie jumped in. "I read about it in a magazine." She stood with one hand on the mantelpiece, her face as gray as the ashes in the grate; Bobby stood beside her vacant-faced, his shoulders rounded and his arms swinging as he attempted to look as young and dimwitted as possible. Dulcie forced a smile and said, "Isn't that where that Griffin man makes all those flickers?"

It was a valiant try and her instincts were right—some knowledge was less suspect than complete ignorance—but McCoy did not buy it. "Yeah, sure," he said, narrowing his eyes. He walked over to Dulcie and grabbed her wrist. Dulcie dropped her eyes and moaned softly.

"Unhand my wife, sir!" C.J. cried.

"This little girlie is married to you?" the man sneered. "Who's this," he jerked a thumb at Bobby, "yer kid?"

C.J. crossed the room quickly, crowded in between Dulcie and Bobby, and put his arms around their shoulders. "Now, see here, McCoy," he said heatedly. "I've had just about enough. You come into my home, you turn it upside down, you insult my family and friends. You, sir, are no gentleman!"

The tension in the room was palpable. Miranda wanted very badly to laugh—the Boss was rarely guilty of understatement—but fought off the impulse by biting her thumb until the fold between her teeth turned white.

"Lissen," McCoy hissed. "You—"

Boom! Boom! Boom! This time everyone jumped, McCoy included. The Widow let out a shriek and clutched her throat. McCoy

flung free Dulcie's wrist and strode to the door. "What the Sam Hill was that?" he bellowed.

"Woodbox," came the shouted answer. Suddenly Miranda remembered the story about her mama's father; how, as a little boy, he had hidden in the root cellar while General Sherman passed overhead on the March to the Sea. I know this isn't a real war, she thought, but I'll bet that's what cannon fire sounds like.

McCoy turned and leaned against the wall. "Tight-lipped pack a liars, ain't ya?" he said, and sucked his teeth. "I can see I'm not gonna get much outta ya." He smiled grimly. "My men'll get what I need, though, you can bet on it."

A mannequin fell in the sewing room, followed by a burst of harsh laughter, and the footsteps pounded away into the dining room. China crashed, and Mary and Lucy moaned as one. "Whadja get?" "Pitcher on the table." Mary whispered, "That was a wedding present from my mother," and buried her face in her hands. Lucy reached across The Widow and patted her, soothing, "There there, honey. There, there."

"Hey, Al," called a voice in the cellar. "Down here!"

McCoy pointed a warning finger at C.J. "Don't you go nowhere," he said, and slipped into the hall.

"What a boor that man is," Lucy whispered.

"A boor?" C.J. whispered harshly. "He approaches Neanderthal. I can't—"

"Turner!" McCoy yelled from the hall; they met in the doorway. "Mind tellin' me," he said coolly, "what all that canvas is for?"

Panic had C.J.'s adrenaline running high. "Boating, my good man!" he cried. "Boating on the mighty Matawan. Ah, to feel your hand on the tiller, wind in your hair."

"So where's the boat, my good man?" was the acid response.

C.J. glanced over his shoulder, then said in a low voice, "Sank. Like the proverbial stone. Don't say anything in front of Mrs. Arnold. She's still in mourning for the lil' doggie."

McCoy turned and roared, *"We're leavin'."* He stepped to the center of the doorway and gave one last disgusted look around the room. "My men tell me there ain't so much as one frame of film in this joint—but don't think you pulled the wool over the eagle eyes of Slim McCoy fer good. I can smell an independent from a mile away." He looked sideways at C.J. and sneered, "And I can smell a director from two." He tipped his hat and said sourly, "Good day, ladies." He turned on his heel, then paused and looked back at C.J. "If the one in black really is yer mother-in-law you got worse trouble than the Trust."

Miranda balanced the plate of sandwiches on the back of the sofa and tiptoed to the window. The car accelerated down the block and took the corner on two wheels. "They're gone," she announced. "Whew!"

Dulcie grabbed the mantel and said, "I can't stop shaking," in a high tight voice. C.J. strode over to Miranda, and jerked aside the curtains. "A curse be on your house, McCoy!" he roared out the window, his face reddening. "May your camels all die! May your tents all blow away! May your children all . . . be . . . *actors!*"

And Miranda heard, coming faintly from across the street, a voice shrieking, "Hobart, those trashy people are at it again. Hobart? Hobart!"—and the sound of a window slamming down.

"Mercy," said Lucy. "Well, let's get some of this mess cleaned up." She stood, folded her arms, and said to C.J., "Before this day ends you and I are going to have a little talk. There is a great deal left unsaid here, a great deal. . . ."

Miranda and Bobby had been banished to the backyard. The sun was low behind the trees. The air was mellow and warm, but with a slight tang, the first winey hint of autumn. Miranda heard a noise and looked up; a flock of birds was V-ing blindly to the South. Summer was ending, she realized, and the sad tightness from that morning flooded her chest.

Bobby leaned on one elbow and watched the fireflies wink their intermittent dance over the bushes. "Didja see The Widow's face

when Dulce gave her what-for?" he said dreamily. "If I live to be a hundred I'll never forget it."

If I live to be a hundred I'll never forget you, she thought. "Bobby? You wanna be blood brothers?" There was no reply. She saw the moody expression and thought, I guess it's another game he never played. "You cut your fingers," she explained, "and mix the blood. Blood brothers, see?"

"Uh-huh," he said. "You fall on me, you bite me, you almost drown me, you get me to lie for you, and now you wanna cut me open." He laughed, and poked her foot. "You are one dangerous female, Miranda Gaines!"

She looked at the silhouetted heads moving back and forth in the lighted kitchen window. "I guess they're talking about me," she sighed.

"You guess," he snorted. "What else would they be talkin' about? The political situation in Europe?" He paused, then said, "There's one thing I never did get straight. How did your aunt see *Cupid*?"

"When we got to the theater yesterday for my birthday treat *Quo Vadis* had burned up in some fire, the manager said, so they ran it instead. They—"

"Eeee-yah!" Bobby hooted. "You mean you two were sittin' there and— What a scene that must've been! Aaah!" He fell back and rolled shrieking in the grass like a puppy let off its chain.

"It's not funny," she said, her voice trembling. "It was awful. I thought I was gonna die on the spot, but then—"

Bobby sat up and brushed off his pants. "Then what? Come on, Red. Spill."

"Well, Auntie figured out who The Little Sister was and she dragged me home and I didn't even get to see the rest of the picture—" Gossamer images swam against the trees. "Oh, Bobby," she said, her eyes shining, "it was so wonderful I forgot to be scared. It was like— Oh, it was like I was part of the screen and the music

and everyone in the theater. Everything we did came true. I think I understand now, all the things C.J. said."

"All that clobber about the soul, and hopes and dreams?" he said, and smiled at her. "You have to see it for yourself to understand. C.J.'s hard to take sometimes, but if he wasn't talented we wouldn't've left steady jobs to work with him. He believes in moving pictures, more'n any of us." He wound a hand in his hair and said, "I do it 'cause I know how, mostly. It's something I learned early, imagining. It's—it's easier for me in front of the camera. Safer there . . . maybe 'cause I can be someone else." He turned his head and their eyes met. "But you *gotta* be in pictures, Red, you're a natural. You're—you're really good."

She stared at him: a compliment?

As always, he took refuge behind a quip. "Aw, where else're you gonna go?—someone who goes through life with one foot on a banana peel and the other in her mouth."

"Bob-beee!"

"Ow! All right, I deserved that one." He rubbed his arm and moaned in overacted agony.

"Why do you always have to tease me?"

"Because I like teasing you. . . . okay?"

"Okay . . . Bobby?" The feeling in the pit of her stomach told her what the answer would be but she could hold it in no longer. "What's going to happen to the Company? Is C.J. going to do another picture here?"

"He wanted to," he said soberly. "I don't know now. My guess is we'll move on, farther away from Fort Lee and the City. The Trust'll be keeping some eye on us after this. It worked for today, but I'm not so sure about tomorrow."

"School starts in two weeks," she whispered. I've read about broken hearts in books, she thought. I bet this is what it feels like. "Will you write to me wherever you go?" she said sadly.

"I've never been much of one for letter-writing," Bobby said huskily, "but I guess it wouldn't kill me."

Miranda rested her face on her knees. "Bobby?" she murmured. "I'll never forget you. Promise me you won't forget me?"

Once again the endearingly lopsided smile caught at her. "Aw, Red, how could I? I'll always have the bruises— Ow! And the scars— Ow! Jeez, cut it out! I was joshin', for cripes sake. Oh, Miranda, please don't cry. I won't forget you."

"Ever?" came the muffled whisper.

"Ever."

Aunt Lucy

The supper dishes were washed and dried and put away. Miranda folded the dish towel and hung it on the hook by the sink. I feel like that poor rag, she thought, I really do. All wrinkly and damp and wrung-out. Oh, what a day.

"Let's go out front and get a breath of air," said Lucy. "I have to talk to you, and it's stifling in here."

Miranda shuffled down the hall behind her, drooped into the swing, and hugged a cushion to her chest. Here it comes, she thought glumly. The lecture of all time followed by the punishment of all time . . . she probably won't even let me write to Bobby.

"We haven't been doing very well lately, have we?" Lucy began. "It doesn't speak well for either of us, that I was so easily lied to. Oh, honey, I'm not the enemy. I'm the one person you could have come to. The one person who would've understood." She pulled a leaf off a geranium and rolled it around in the palm of one hand until it was a wet green ball.

She's not yelling at me, Miranda thought. She's not even looking at me. Auntie always looks you right in the eye when she talks to you, even when you wish she wouldn't.

Lucy dropped the green lump on the wicker table beside the swing. She seemed riveted to the magazine on the table, stroking the shiny cover absentmindedly. Miranda glanced over; what was so fascinating about the May issue of *The Delineator*?

"I had a crazy summer once," Lucy said, finally. "The summer I was seventeen. I ran away from home. . . . I don't know why I'm telling you this when I should be taking a switch to you, but it seems to fit." The slender fingers traced figure eights. "I ran away with a friend. We toured vaudeville."

Mademoiselle Lucille! thought Miranda.

"We sang all the old songs," Lucy went on. "We got some decent bookings, a few split weeks. It wasn't much of an act, but we made a pretty picture. He wore tails—oh, he was so elegant!—and I had a pink dress, all ruffles. Tiny diamonds down the front. . . . I made it myself, too, sitting cross-legged on my bed, shoving it under the pillow every time I heard footsteps in the hall."

She smiled impishly; and suddenly Miranda saw her as she must have been that summer, saw her as clearly as if C.J. had projected the image on a painted wall. She saw the dress, too; not crumpled and stained and hidden in a dark attic, but fresh and crisp and silken, the crystals sewn in secret catching the upward glow of the footlights as a tiny-waisted blond girl dipped and swirled and sang, her curls piled high, her cheeks pink.

"I found the dress," Miranda whispered. "It's the most beautiful dress I ever saw."

"Yes," said Lucy, her eyes still on the magazine, "I could always sew." Her expression sharpened slightly. "You found it?" she said, then smiled. "Oh, well, it doesn't matter now, does it . . . sometimes I can't believe it really happened. All those towns, the trains in the middle of the night, the shabby hotels, the cramped dressing rooms— Oh, how I loved it! I loved every minute of it. . . . You should see your face. Pretty racy stuff for your old auntie, eh?

You're not the only one with greasepaint in your veins, you know." She laughed, and walked over and sat down next to Miranda.

"But, Aunt Lucy, I don't understand," Miranda said. "Bobby did that—he was in the theater—and he positively hated it. He said it was horrible and lonely, and you make it sound like some sort of adventure."

"It's not an easy life, honey," she replied. "If he told you that he was right. You have to love it; the work and the people. I suspect you've already found that out. And my friend—Curtis was his name, Curtis Jameson—oh, he had a smile that would lift your heart and break it all at once. He was a lot like your Bobby." She saw the glow on the girl's face and thought, He may very well turn out to be "your Bobby," you just don't know it yet—which is as it should be.

"Auntie?" Why do grownups do that? she thought impatiently, stop just when it's getting interesting. "What happened next? Tell me the rest of the story."

"The rest of the story. Well, Mama and Papa found us in St. Louis around the end of August, and there was the worst shouting match I have ever heard. It wasn't so much that I had run away, or even that I had run off with Curtis. I had *lied* to them," she said pointedly, and Miranda flushed uncomfortably. "So they dragged me home and that was the end of it. No more vaudeville. Your father tried to defend me, but he was no more than a child himself, and Papa never listened to him anyway. Then Mama got sick and I took care of her, and then Papa . . . and then I started teaching, and here I am. End of story."

Miranda waited for a bit, then asked, very carefully, "What happened to your friend?"

Lucy looked away somewhere into the distance, and her gray eyes brimmed with tears. "Papa paid him off, I suppose."

Politely, so as not to appear overly interested in Lucy's tears, Miranda looked out over the lawn. The streetlamps were on. The sky was a rich shade of sapphire, somewhere between the wisteria

drowsing over the end of the porch and Dulcie's eyes. After the handkerchief had been returned to Lucy's sleeve, Miranda said, "Then you don't hate theater people after all?"

Lucy stood, straightened her skirt, and patted smooth the back of her pompadour. She folded her arms at her waist and looked down at her niece with some amusement. "You just don't think things through much, do you? Did it ever occur to you that I am a single woman raising a child alone—and Lord, what a child!—and our livelihood depends on my reputation as a clean-living, God-fearing woman?"

"O-o-o-oh," said Miranda.

"Yes," said Lucy drily. "Oh. So I have to keep on the good side of people like Emma Duncan whether I want to or not. Let's go get some lemonade. All this talk has made me thirsty."

They chipped ice into tall glasses, and sliced lemons, and stirred sugar. Like a sailor surveying the horizon for clouds building to the south, Miranda kept glancing at Lucy. When was she going to yell at her? For that matter, when was she going to talk about C.J.? I could get it out of him tomorrow, she thought, but if I have to wait 'til then I *will* die.

They returned to the porch with the frosty glasses. Lucy perched on the railing, tilted her head back against the post, and swung one foot as she sipped. Miranda curled up in the swing and stared at her with the intensity of Slim McCoy.

Lucy turned her head. "You really are the beatenest child," she laughed. "Do you honestly think I can't tell what's going on in that head of yours?"

"Jerry says I've got a naked face," Miranda said. I guess I'm not such a great actress after all, she thought.

Lucy looked off into the twilight and said, quietly, "I was born in this house. I don't know if I can leave it."

Miranda froze, the glass at her mouth. "What are you talking about?" she said in a choked whisper.

"Oh, as if you haven't been thinking of little else." Lucy pulled

her spectacles from her skirt pocket and put them on, then took another look at Miranda's face. "For heaven's sake," she said. "He didn't tell you, did he. California. Mr. Tourneur's taking the Company to California."

Miranda made a face and said, "Oh, that. He's always talking about California. California and D. W. Griffith. We just let him rattle on when he gets like that."

Lucy rolled the glass across her forehead and sighed, "My, it certainly is warm this evening."

"Auntie!"

"All right, Miss Know-It-All. Apparently what happened today made up his mind. He's going West and he wants to put you under contract. Something about more pictures with The Little Sister character, but I'm not sure I got it straight, he does go on—"

"They're not jus' going to another town? We're goin' out West with—I can't believe it! I knew it, I knew it, I just knew you'd like them, they're the best people ever in the whole entire world, the best friends I . . . ever . . . had." She threw herself back onto the cushions. "Oof!"

"I did not say we were going," Lucy said with biting deliberation. "I said we had been asked to go. I told him we would think about it. It would mean giving up everything here, moving lock, stock, and barrel all the way across the country—and I'm not so sure about that man's business meth— Miranda, have you heard one word I've said? Stop it, you'll spill that."

Miranda was up and off the swing, zigzagging an intoxicated dance of joy down the porch, braid flying. I'll make her go, she thought wildly, if I have to tie her up to get her on the train. I'll talk her into it, I'll make Bobby help me. I'll get C.J. to talk to her some more—he could talk anybody into anything. . . . I better not tell her he still owes me a whole summer's worth of dollar-a-day, though.

She reined in beside Lucy and a splash of lemonade leapt from the glass. She grabbed her aunt's arm. "Oh, please, Auntie, please,"

she panted. "I have to go to California, I have to be in pictures, Bobby says I'm a natural. I promise I'll be good. I'll make my bed and not sass back and never give you any more trouble, cross-my-heart-and-hope-to-die-stick-a-needle-in-my-eye."

"I rather doubt that," Lucy said drily.

"Please, Aunt Lucy," she said as solemnly as she could, given her pounding heart and cottony mouth. "You must know how I feel. You wanted adventure too, didn't you?"

Lucy looked at the bright face and thought, Oh, Lordy, what am I going to do? One summer of glory, then just memories? I want better for her than that. "I'll think about it, darling," she said wearily. "That's all I can promise for now."

Mr. Fellowes walked down the sidewalk and, as usual, tipped his hat. They waved and smiled and returned his greeting. Lucy leaned back and looked out at the quiet street. I've lived my whole life here, she thought. I know the insides of my neighbors' houses as well as my own . . . maybe we could try it for six months. I suppose I could lease the house and find someone to take my students for that long, and they must need dresses and piano lessons out there. All the way across a continent. All that way for a crazy business peopled with lunatics. I must be mad to even consider it.

Suddenly Emma Duncan's doughy face flashed across her mind. She grinned and thought, Emma will—what's Miranda's phrase?— Emma will 'just die.' Oh darling girl, my dear brother certainly knew what he was doing when he took your name from *The Tempest.*

Miranda stood at the top of the porch steps. She saw neither the wide-browed houses with their welcoming porches, nor the tall trees sheltering the broad lawns and the dusty street. She saw the fierce aquamarine of a Western sky, arched over a shore trembling under breakers rolling in all the way from China. She saw cactus, and C.J. thwacking a riding crop against his breeches as he strode, bellowing, through desert scrub. She saw Bobby, tall and brave on a horse, his black curls smoothed under a ten-gallon hat.

She saw a touring car of the palest lemon yellow pull up to the grand high gates of a studio. A glamorous figure lounged against the plush seat, toying with the yellow rosebud in the crystal vase on the doorjamb. A chauffeur in yellow livery got out to open the back door. With autograph books and fountain pens at the ready, the waiting crowd whispered excitedly: "Who is that?" "Aw, don't you know nuthin'? That's Miranda Gaines!" "Say, if she ain't the swellest thing to ever cross the silversheet!"

Miranda Gaines, Star of the Silver Screen, stood on the running board. She spread wide her arms to greet her adoring public—and to display her new lemon velvet gown, the one with the six-foot train. The glass of lemonade crashed down the steps and shattered, the splintery shards twinkling in the fading light.

"Miranda!"

JANE KENDALL has written on social history for a variety of publications; her illustration credits include *Petrouchka: A Ballet Cutout Book* and *The Nutcracker: A Ballet Cutout Book*. She is a graduate of the American Musical and Dramatic Academy. Ms. Kendall lives in Cos Cob, Connecticut, where she collects vintage hats and stays up late most nights watching old films.